"You're beautiful," he said quietly

When he continued, Wyatt's voice was professionally detached. "Most of my patients are uncertain about their appearance and lack the confidence to accomplish anything positive."

"Is that why you kissed me?" Cassie demanded.

Wyatt pressed his lips tightly together while formulating a harmless explanation. "It should never have happened," he said finally. "I would be lying if I asked you to believe that I didn't respond to you—on a very basic level. But that response has no place in our relationship as a doctor and patient. Do you understand?"

"No."

He exhaled sharply in exasperation. "Just think of it as a mistake. A mistake that won't happen again."

Cassie lowered her eyes and nodded. On the table Wyatt's hand had tightened into a fist of white tension....

WELCOME
TO THE WONDERFUL WORLD
OF *Harlequin Presents*

Interesting, informative and entertaining,
each Harlequin Presents portrays an appealing
and original love story. With a varied array
of settings, we may lure you on an African safari,
to a quaint Welsh village, or an exotic Riviera
location—anywhere and everywhere that adventurous
men and women fall in love.

As publishers of Harlequin Presents, we're
extremely proud of our books. Since 1949,
Harlequin Enterprises has built its publishing
reputation on the solid base of quality and
originality. Our stories are the most popular
paperback romances sold in North America; every
month, eight new titles are released and sold at
nearly every book-selling store in Canada and the
United States.

For a list of all titles currently available,
send your name and address to:

HARLEQUIN READER SERVICE,
(In the U.S.) P.O. Box 52040, Phoenix, AZ 85072-2040
(In Canada) P.O. Box 2800, Postal Station A,
5170 Yonge Street, Willowdale, Ont. M2N 6J3

We sincerely hope you enjoy reading
this Harlequin Presents.

Yours truly,

THE PUBLISHERS
Harlequin Presents

MELINDA CROSS

lion of darkness

Harlequin Books

TORONTO • NEW YORK • LONDON
AMSTERDAM • PARIS • SYDNEY • HAMBURG
STOCKHOLM • ATHENS • TOKYO • MILAN

Harlequin Presents first edition January 1986
ISBN 0-373-10847-8

Original hardcover edition published in 1985
by Mills & Boon Limited

CHAPTER ONE

PARK AVENUE always sounded the same in the morning. A thousand different sounds joined in the rumble of the giant city coming to life, and Cassandra Winters loved them all.

She stood at the entrance of the glass and steel highrise, wisps of pale, blonde hair moving with the morning breeze, her head cocked, listening. She separated the delighted squeals of children playing in Central Park from the sounds of traffic, and smiled.

She was still smiling when a young man walked past, emitting a long, low whistle. She opened large blue eyes to the glare of the morning, and her smile grew. 'It's a crude expression of appreciation,' her father had told her. 'A compliment, in an irritating sort of way.'

But Cassie didn't think it was irritating. She needed every assurance of her presentability she could get. And even that didn't always help. She still thought of herself as ugly, disfigured, and all of her father's praise had done little to dispel the feeling. He was her father, after all. He would have to think she was beautiful.

'Miss Cassie! I'm so sorry. I didn't see you come down.'

'It's all right, Robert. I'm perfectly comfortable here.' She smiled fondly in the general direction of the elderly doorman. He'd been a part of her life as long as she could remember, too. Just like the sounds of New York City.

'I know, Miss Cassie. But your father doesn't like you out here alone ... oh, I'm sorry, Miss. I keep forgetting.'

'I know, Robert,' she said gently. 'I do too.'

'Such a fine man, he was,' Robert mused. 'It's hard to think of him being gone. And so quick, too. But then

I suppose it's better that way. Ah, here comes your car now, Miss Cassie. You're sure about this, are you?'

'Yes, Robert.'

She counted two steps down to the sidewalk, then seven more across to the kerb.

'Your father was against it, you know,' he added uncertainly.

'My father worried about me too much, Robert. He's dead now. I have to learn to take care of myself. And high time, too, I'd say. I must be the only twenty-five-year-old in the world with a live-in babysitter.'

'Ah, Miss, it's not like that . . .'

'It *is* like that, Robert! It's always been like that!' she said sharply. 'Father took care of me, I took care of Father, and the servants took care of us both. We've been smothering up there for nearly twenty years, and at last, it's going to stop!' She sensed his hurt and reached out with her hand. He grasped it quickly. 'Please don't worry, Robert. I'll feel terrible if you do. And I'll be fine; really I will. I'll write. Once a week, I'll write.'

She moved her hand up his arm to rest on his cheek, and kissed it gently. 'Thank you, Robert; for helping at the funeral; for everything. I'll see you in a few months.'

She thought she felt a tear on her hand as she pulled it away, but she couldn't be sure. She slipped into the back seat of the limousine and heard the chauffeur close the door gently behind her. She turned her face to the glass window and smiled, waving goodbye to Robert, wondering if he were looking. That's the trouble with being blind, she thought. You never know if anyone waves back.

It was two hours up the Hudson to Windrow. Half of that was just getting out of the city, of course, and that was pleasant. There were a million different sounds outside the car, telling a million different stories, and she was never bored as long as there was something to hear. But then the city fell away, and the sameness of the country sounds lulled her to sleep.

She wakened when the car stopped. Well, Cassie, she told herself, that's your last ride in a limousine for a while; maybe forever.

The chauffeur opened the door, helped her out of the car, and put her bags next to her on the sidewalk. 'You're right in front of the main house, Miss,' he said. 'Just up the steps and through the door.' And then he left quickly, almost frantically, as if her blindness were a contagious disease he would catch if exposed for too long. Some people were like that, she knew. Those were the people who made her feel ugly. The people Father had kept shut out, all those years. Mark wasn't like that. Mark would never have left her out here alone, helpless. He would have taken her into the building, found someone to help her, made sure she was settled before he left. But Mark had been the family driver for years, more relative than servant, and she had had to let him go. A week after Father's death she had had to let them all go; all but Mrs Carmody, of course.

So. Just up the stairs and through the door. But which way were the stairs, and how many? Where was the building? Behind her? Beside her?

She cocked her head, listening, hoping to hear the sounds people made. Just one person. Anyone.

She heard the sharp call of a blackbird, thrown across an open space; a door slamming far away, miles away, it seemed, and her shoulders slumped in frustration. She sidled carefully to her right in short, mincing steps until her foot bumped against her bags. She bent from the waist and felt for her largest case, then sat carefully on its edge.

'Terrific,' she said aloud, just to hear the sound of a human voice. 'A school for the blind and there's no one here to even help me up the steps.'

'Why don't you help yourself?' The voice came from far above her, over her left shoulder, and she jumped up in alarm, knocking her suitcase on its side.

'Who is it? Who's there?'

'I said,' the voice persisted, 'why don't you help yourself?'

She straightened to her full height, lifting her chin imperiously. 'And I said, who's there?' she demanded.

There was no answer for a moment. When the voice spoke again, she could hear the smile. 'Wyatt Field is here.'

'Well,' she exhaled with relief. 'Thank goodness. I was beginning to think the place was deserted. Since there doesn't seem to be anyone else about, perhaps you'd be good enough to help me.'

'I'd be happy to help you. That's my job. Just tell me how.'

She liked his voice. He'd be a bass; no, a baritone, she decided. Deep, but mellow.

'Well,' she replied in a businesslike tone, 'for starters you could help me up the stairs and into the building. And then there's my luggage.'

'Leave your luggage,' he said firmly. 'Someone will see to it later. And as for help up the stairs, you look like a reasonably healthy young woman. I watched you use both legs, so I know you're not crippled. You can get up the stairs yourself.'

She smiled with familiar tolerance, closing her eyes briefly. 'I'm afraid you don't understand, Mr Field. I'm blind.'

His voice came back steady and commanding. 'Maybe. But like I said, not crippled.'

'You mean you *knew* I was blind?' Her voice was shrill.

'Of course.'

'And you stood there all that time watching, and didn't help me?'

'I'm sitting, not standing, and everyone here is blind. Except for the staff, of course. If the few sighted people that live here spent all their time leading the blind around, we wouldn't have time for anything else.'

She spluttered in frustration, then nearly shrieked at

him, 'Don't lecture me! I know the blind are supposed to be independent here! That's why I came. But I've only just arrived. I would think you could make a few concessions to at least get me in the door!'

Her lower lip quivered in complete contrast to the haughty set of her chin, and the man at the top of the stairs frowned. This was always the hardest part. Watching them try to get up the stairs.

'All right. I'll make a concession. The stairs are directly in front of you.'

'How many?'

'I've never counted them.'

Anger set her lips in a hard line, and she tossed her head. The sun caught the burnished light of her long, almost colourless hair as it flew across her shoulder, and Wyatt Field suppressed a whistle. She had beautiful hair. He wondered if she knew it.

She began to shuffle slowly forward, her arms extended stiffly from the shoulders.

'Don't do that!' he commented. 'Put your arms down! You look like a blind person!'

'I *am* a blind person!' she shrilled back.

'That doesn't mean you have to look like one! Now put your arms down. There's nothing in front of you. Trust me.'

'Trust you? I may be blind, Mr Field, but I'm not crazy!'

The sound of his deep laughter infuriated her. She moved steadily forward, a little faster now, until her toe bumped the first step. She climbed slowly, tapping the back of each step with her toe, counting automatically, and sensed his presence to her left when she reached nine. She stomped one foot lightly, listening to the sound. She was on the porch.

The corners of her lips turned up in a smug smile of accomplishment, and she went forward slowly, her arms extended in defiance, until her hands touched the building. She let them drop slowly to waist level, then roam back and forth until they found the knob of a door. She turned it, pushed in, and walked through, smiling broadly. She heard his hands coming together in slow, mocking applause behind her.

'Well, for Heaven's sake! It must be Miss Winters! Oh my, I'm so sorry!' A bright-sounding young woman hustled towards her across the wide foyer. 'Oh, Miss Winters, I don't know what to say. I should have been watching for you, but the time has just flown this morning. I lost track of it altogether. Let me look at you.'

Small, firm hands grasped her shoulders gently, holding her at arms' length. 'My, my. You are a beauty, aren't you? Oh, listen to me ramble, you just in and lost as a lamb, I'm sure. The name's Maggie, Maggie O'Shea, and I'm as flame-haired Irish as the name sounds.'

'Are you a teacher? A doctor?' Cassie asked softly, a bit overcome by the exuberance of the chattering woman, but grateful for a friendly voice.

'Me? Oh my, no. I'm sort of a housemother. Although in your case, since we're about the same age, a housesister. It's my job to welcome the guests, make them feel at home, help them adjust, if I can. I'm sort of the listening ear here, in lieu of the friendly face, although I'm told I have one of those, too. A shoulder to cry on, if you need one; that sort of thing. Ah, Dr Field! There you are!'

Cassie's smile faded. 'Dr Field?'

'Ah, you've met then. I suppose it was Dr Field who helped you in.'

'Helped me in?' Cassie's voice was incredulous. 'I'm just grateful he didn't stick out a foot to trip me on my way up the stairs.'

Maggie winked over Cassie's head to Field's smile, but made her voice scold. 'Oh, he's a one, he is! Dr Field, you expect too much too soon. You always do.'

'What does he look like?' Cassie asked impulsively.

Field's eyebrows raised and he inclined his head to Maggie.

'What do *you* think he looks like?' Maggie asked, her round, rosy face lifting with a smile. She loved this part. The newcomers, still smarting from Wyatt's seemingly cold indifference during their first trip up at the front steps, usually imagined him with horns and warts.

Cassie hesitated, then turned on her heel. Her hands found his chest directly in front of her, as she knew they would, and fluttered over his torso and his face in a light, cursory inspection. They rested momentarily on his cheeks, and she felt him tense before dropping her arms to her sides. 'He's six foot two,' she said without hesitation, 'black hair, blue eyes, I think; large ones for a man, with thick lashes. Square chin, strong, with a dimple. Straight, finely-shaped nose. Quite handsome, I would guess, with those high cheekbones. And he played football some time ago. Quarterback,' she concluded.

There was a brief silence, then his voice. 'How old am I, Miss Winters?'

She touched her fingers to her lips, frowning. 'Thirty. No. Thirty-one.'

Maggie's laugh trilled and echoed in the large, empty area. 'Well, there you are Wyatt. What do you have to say now?'

'Was I close, Maggie?' Cassie asked. 'And don't humour me—my father used to do that when I was still learning. It's the cruellest thing of all.'

Maggie's cheerful face softened and a tiny line of sympathy marked her forehead. 'We know that, Miss Winters. We don't humour the blind here. Not ever. You were almost exactly right, except he's probably more handsome than you imagined, aren't you, Wyatt?' Her voice was playful again. 'He's a real ladykiller, he is. But how did you know about his eyes? Once you knew his hair was black, you should have guessed dark eyes.'

'His voice is too cold for dark eyes,' Cassie answered. 'I knew that the first time he spoke to me.'

CHAPTER TWO

MAGGIE showed her to her room, one flight up, three doors down the wide hall, and helped her acquaint herself with the placing of the furniture.

'It seems odd, Maggie,' Cassie said as she sagged to the soft double bed.' There are so many stairs here. I'd think a school for the blind would be all on one floor. Especially one with this reputation. Lord knows your prices are high enough to pay for remodelling.'

Maggie laughed gently. 'There are stairs in the real world, Miss Winters. Lots of them. The most important thing we do at Windrow is teach you to live comfortably with all the things that frighten you on the outside. Eliminating the obstacles wouldn't do much good, now, would it?'

'No, I suppose not.'

'Now then. You should hang your own clothes so you know where to find things; otherwise you'll be mixing your outfits.'

Cassie hesitated, her lips pressed together in embarrassment.

'What is it?'

'I don't know much about my clothes—colours, and so on. Mrs Carmody always laid them out for me . . . and helped me dress,' she added softly.

A low whistle escaped Maggie's full lips. 'My Lord, girl. What *have* you learned to do for yourself?'

Cassie stiffened and blinked rapidly. 'Nothing, Maggie. Absolutely nothing. That's why I'm here.'

Maggie gathered a file folder from the night stand next to the bed, and pulled a pen from behind her ear. 'It's all right—Cassie, isn't it? Not to worry. You'll learn in jig time. Now let's get some of this down, so your teachers will have something to go on. I'm afraid your Mrs Carmody was a bit sketchy when she called to register you. When were you blinded, Cassie?'

'When I was seven.' She heard the scratching of Maggie's pen on paper.

'How?'

'Car accident, or so they tell me. I don't remember the crash at all. Some times before that, and everything after, but not being in the car, not the accident, nothing.' She caught her lower lip between her teeth for a moment, then continued. 'My mother was killed.'

Maggie made an automatic sound of sympathy, and kept writing. 'Are your medical records being transferred here?'

'Yes, Mrs Carmody arranged that, but there aren't many. I haven't seen a doctor in nearly ten years. I'm ridiculously healthy.'

Maggie looked up sharply and frowned, her grey eyes suddenly dark. 'That's a long time between examinations, Cassie. What did he tell you? About your sight, I mean.'

Cassie's eyes brimmed automatically, and she opened them wide and tipped her head back to keep the tears inside. 'That there was no physiological reason for my blindness—hysterical blindness, he called it. That my eyes were fine, but my mind simply refused to see.'

Maggie nodded sagely, as if she heard that every day. 'What else?'

Cassie took a deep breath, then exhaled with a shudder. 'That I should see a psychiatrist.'

'And did you?'

'Of course!' she snapped. 'You think I want to be blind? Oh, Maggie. I'm sorry. I didn't mean to be sharp. It's just so frustrating. For the last ten years I've been telling myself I could see, and wondering why the world was still black.'

'It's all right, Cassie,' Maggie soothed. 'Why not tell me the rest? Take your time. There's no hurry here.'

Cassie sighed deeply, then clasped her hands together in her lap. 'I saw the psychiatrist; once a week for nearly a year. It was . . . painful. Father fought it every step of the way. He hated for me to be upset; but I went anyway. The doctor finally said I wasn't emotionally equipped to face whatever trauma had caused my blindness. That I would have to mature; become more self-assured. He recommended this school.'

'Almost ten years ago? And you didn't come until now?' Maggie asked in disbelief. She shook her head, setting her bright red curls bobbing.

'My father was a bit . . . protective,' she explained. 'He couldn't see the sense in coming to a school that taught me how to be blind, when my sight would eventually return. And besides that . . .' she hesitated.

'Yes?'

'. . . besides that, he had a very hard time dealing with my blindness. He couldn't accept it at all. He was so guilty, you see, about the accident. My mother dead, me blind . . . for a while, he wouldn't even say the word "blind" aloud. As if by denying its reality, he could make it go away. Sending me to Windrow would have been an admission that I couldn't see.'

'I take it your father was driving when you had the accident,' Maggie interjected drily.

'Yes. So to his way of thinking, everything that happened was his responsibility. The guilt destroyed him; emotionally, that is. We had an estate on the Hudson, not too far from here. My mother loved that house.' Cassie paused and smiled, remembering something pleasant; then the smile faded and she straightened on the bed. 'Anyway, Father closed it up and bought the penthouse before I even got out of the hospital. He couldn't stand the house without Mother, I suppose, and thought the penthouse would be easier for me—no stairs, no river, no danger.' Her voice trailed off, then came back stronger, as if she had regained control. 'I never even got to go home. And that was only the beginning. He was determined that I would never know the frustration most blind people face. It became an obsession with him. He hired servants to be my eyes. To dress me, to cook for me, to take me to the park, to dial the phone, to read to me. Everything.'

'You mean you never learned braille?' Maggie interrupted in amazement.

Cassie nodded, smiling. 'That was his only concession, and our only really big argument. Learning braille was just another acknowledgment that I was blind; like seeing the psychiatrist. But eventually he gave in, hired a tutor, and I learned that much, at least.'

'A tutor?'

'Of course. I rarely left the penthouse. Except to go across the street to the park. With a chaperon.'

Maggie set her pen down and tried to keep the anger out of her voice. 'So for all practical purposes, you've been a prisoner for the last eighteen years. Locked away. Safe.'

'Don't say it like that, Maggie. He didn't mean any harm.'

'They never do.' She sighed deeply and stood. 'So why did he finally give in and send you here?'

'He didn't. He died. Two weeks ago.'

'I'm sorry,' Maggie said quickly. 'I didn't realise . . .' She hesitated lamely. 'You wanted to come years ago, didn't you?' she asked kindly.

'Yes. Very much.'

'But you didn't want to put your father through it.'

'Something like that,' Cassie mumbled.

Maggie passed a hand over eyes suddenly tired. 'I have a hard time understanding sacrifice like that, Cassie. So will most of the people here. You'll have to be patient with us. But no matter. At least you're here now, and you've got your work cut out for you. Now then!' Her voice changed immediately, and she was bright and professional once again. 'There'll be medical examinations first; this afternoon, tomorrow too, if the doctors need more time. Then you'll start right in with Dr Field.'

Cassie straightened, immediately wary. 'Dr Field? Why him? Aren't there other teachers?'

Maggie chuckled in understanding. 'I know how he seems at first, and he'll probably seem worse as time goes on. But most of our students leave here loving him.'

Cassie grunted sceptically.

'He's the staff psychiatrist,' Maggie continued. 'Everyone who comes here spends the first two weeks with him. As a matter of fact, you'll hardly see anyone else, except for me, of course. Think of it as an initiation. It'll be over before you know it. Now. Let's get you some lunch, then off to the doctors, shall we?'

Maggie was as solicitous as Dr Field had been indifferent. She guided Cassie carefully down the broad, curving staircase, her hand cupping Cassie's elbow in protective reassurance. She described every detail of the areas they passed through on the way to the dining room, emphasising the particulars of architecture Cassie would use later as directional guideposts; a banister here, a window seat there.

'The entrance to the dining room is flanked by two fern stands,' Maggie informed her. 'One on either side of the door. We're almost there now. Can you smell them?'

'Oh yes. Boston ferns, aren't they?'

Maggie's brows peaked momentarily. 'That they are,' she answered with surprise. 'Was that a lucky guess?'

'No, of course not. The Boston fern has a very distinctive odour. All plants do, actually. Father kept a small greenhouse on the roof, and lectured me endlessly on plant identification. I'm pretty good at it.'

'Well,' Maggie responded, mysteriously, 'you'll be a jump ahead of most of our students. The plants are just about the only thing Wyatt refuses to move around here.'

'What do you mean?'

'Never mind. You'll learn soon enough. Straight ahead now. There's a clear centre aisle, about ten feet wide. The tables seat four people, and there are sixteen of them, eight on each side. We have the place to ourselves today, so you can wander a moment. Get the feel of the room. Bump your shins a few times, then sit where you like.'

Cassie's hand grasped for Maggie, closing around a sturdy forearm with an urgent pressure. 'You aren't leaving me, are you?'

'No, no,' Maggie reassured her, patting the hand that held her arm captive. 'I'll be right here watching. Go on, now.'

Cassie shuffled forward hesitantly, the natural grace of her slender body distorted by the awkward stiffness of uncertainty, her arms extended at shoulder height.

'Your hands won't help much up that high, Cassie,' Maggie called after her. 'Not here, and not anywhere else in the world either. Most of the obstacles you'll encounter, like the tables and chairs in this room, are only hip-high. You're missing them.'

Cassie dropped her hands obediently in response to the logic of Maggie's statement, and immediately encountered an object she identified as a chair back. She would have missed it with her arms held unnaturally high, and would have stumbled, or cracked her shins at the very least.

How basic, she thought ruefully. How very simple and sensible. Why hadn't anyone ever told her before? And why hadn't Dr Field been as reasonable with the instruction as Maggie; explaining why she should drop her hands instead of simply demanding that she do it without question?

She wandered through the rows of tables with growing confidence, determining their approximate placement in relation to each other.

'Don't bother, Cassie,' Maggie said softly as she walked up behind her.

'Don't bother what?'

'You're memorising the layout. Counting steps between tables; that sort of thing. Save yourself the trouble. It'll all be different by suppertime.'

Cassie turned to face her, amazement dropping her

delicate features into a series of circles that made Maggie smile.

'It's what you came here for, isn't it, Cassie?' she asked gently. 'To learn to deal with the unfamiliar?'

Cassie sank into the closest chair her hands could find and shook her head in dismay. 'Do you mean the furniture is moved *intentionally*? So I won't know where anything is?'

'That's right. That's how you learn. By the time you leave here, you'll be able to walk into all sorts of places you never would have believed you'd risk alone. You may stumble now and then, but the fear will be gone. You'll have confidence in your own ability to deal with the things you can't see.'

Cassie's hands clasped and unclasped on the table before her. 'I don't know if I can go through with it, Maggie,' she whispered. 'I never imagined it would be this hard. Three months here, never knowing where anything is; bumping into things that are never in the same place; getting lost because someone moved the furniture—that's chaos. Even a sighted person would find that disturbing. But for a blind person? It's a nightmare!'

She felt the sympathy emanating from Maggie's hand as it covered hers. 'It won't be as bad as you might think,' she said gently. 'Pretty soon you'll look at it as a challenge, not a terror. Give yourself a little time. Besides,' she continued in a lighter tone, 'there will be some things that won't change. Your room, for instance. That's your sanctuary—like your home would be on the outside. No one will ever move anything in there, except you. And the plants, as I told you. Wyatt refuses to move them ... he says plants aren't as flexible as people, and couldn't stand the disorder.'

'I'm beginning to think the plants have a better chance for survival in this place than I do,' Cassie muttered resentfully.

Maggie only laughed. 'I'm starving, Cassie. How about you? Fill your stomach, empty your mind; that's what my father always said. Here. The menus are in braille.'

Cassie's fingers flew over the menu Maggie pressed into her hand, and her face reflected mild surprise at the selections. 'Very impressive,' she commented. 'This is hardly the cafeteria fare one would expect in a school setting.'

'And this is hardly a cafeteria; or your average school for the blind, for that matter. Surely you know that.'

'I know very little about Windrow, actually. I'd never heard of it until the doctor recommended it, and his description was sketchy, at best. He only said it was excellent. He never even mentioned an alternative, come to think of it. Windrow was apparently the only school he considered suitable.'

'Ah. That tells me more about your family than you can imagine; at least about their financial status. Oh, hello, Helen.'

Cassie heard soft footsteps and the rustle of a lightly starched skirt to her left.

'Hello, Miss O'Shea. And this must be Miss Winters.'

Cassie frowned and interrupted the introductions. 'Am I the only student here?' she asked. 'Everyone seems to know automatically who I am.'

'Wyatt only takes one at a time, Cassie; and devotes his attention to that one student full-time. It seems to be more efficient in the long run, but that's one reason the tuition at Windrow is so prohibitive,' Maggie explained. 'This is Helen, Cassie. She's another of the fixtures around here that's constantly moving. The dining room is her domain; both here, where you'll stay for your two weeks isolation, and at the dormitory, where you'll move later on. She'll serve all your meals, here in the dining room, or in your room if you prefer. She and our chef, Manny, work hand in hand planning and preparing meals, purchasing for the kitchen, and so on.'

'How do you do, Helen,' Cassie greeted her. 'You seem much too young to be labelled as a fixture.'

There was a soft chuckle threaded into a sigh as Helen shook her dark head. 'Thank you, Miss Winters; but I'm not as young as you might think. Voices are deceptive.'

'Watch it, Helen,' Maggie warned her with a smile. 'She's pretty good at age-guessing.'

Helen cocked her head and raised finely arched brows over remarkable dark eyes. 'All right, then. How old am I, Miss Winters?'

Cassie smiled and shrugged. 'It really is a guess without touching you, Helen; but I'd say thirty-three.'

There was a heavy silence, and Cassie frowned, waiting for someone to speak. 'Oh dear,' she said finally. 'I haven't offended you, have I, Helen? It was just a guess, as I told you.'

'I turned thirty-three last week, Miss Winters. You just surprised me, that's all. I should be used to it, I suppose. You people are always surprising me. You know so much more than one would expect.'

Cassie pursed her lips, uncertain of how to respond. She sensed an undercurrent of resentment in Helen's voice; especially when she categorised the blind as 'you people', in a tone that was both derogatory and envious. It was a preposterous notion, of course. How could anyone envy the blind? Cassie shook her head quickly to rid herself of the thought.

'Have you made your selection yet?' Helen's voice was suddenly professional, almost stilted.

'Why don't you choose for us, Helen,' Maggie suggested. 'We put our palates in your hands.'

Cassie was troubled with the uncomfortable thought that she would rather nothing of hers was ever put in Helen's care, but said nothing.

'Very good, Miss O'Shea,' Helen answered formally, and she was gone with a light rustle, leaving the lingering scent of food and a light perfume behind.

'Did I say something wrong, Maggie?' Cassie asked in a low voice, not totally convinced that Helen had left the room. She had a troubling mental picture of the older woman hovering somewhere nearby, watching every move, listening to every word. 'I certainly didn't mean to offend her.'

'No, no. You didn't say anything wrong. Helen's just ... different. Don't be taking anything Helen says or does personally. And don't be imagining trouble where there isn't any, either. Helen has some problems she has to work out for herself, that's all. But they won't affect you, and they don't affect her work. She's really excellent at her job. We're lucky to have her.'

Cassie tipped her head thoughtfully. 'What does she look like?'

'You mean you don't know?' Maggie chided her.

'Not a clue. Not without touching her. And somehow I don't think Helen's the touching type. I'd feel like I was violating the queen, or something.'

Maggie laughed gaily. 'Well, you're certainly right about that. Helen's a very private person. Very proud. And as for her looks, she's what you might call exotic. Almost foreign-looking. Her hair is as black as yours is blonde, and she has the most incredibly large, almond-shaped eyes. Deep brown, I suppose, although they look black too. She's relatively tall, about three inches short of six feet, I think; and she has a bone structure most models would kill for. High, prominent cheek-bones ...'

'Like Dr Field's.'

'More pronounced, but similar, yes.'

'And she's beautiful.'

Maggie paused. 'I guess she is. Darkly beautiful—you know what I mean?'

Cassie shook her head honestly.

'Well, not like you,' Maggie explained earnestly. 'Yours is a fresh, clean, sort of innocent beauty. Helen's is, well ... dark. Secret. Almost tragic.'

Cassie sat perfectly still, her eyes steady, her hands clasped tightly together in her lap.

Maggie noted her rigid posture and frowned. 'What's wrong, Cassie?'

She pressed her lips into a straight, thin line, then released the breath she had been holding. 'What you said,' she whispered. 'About me.'

Maggie's brows nearly touched over her nose. 'About your kind of beauty, you mean? What about it?' She studied Cassie's tightened features until awareness lifted her brows slightly. 'Good Lord. Hasn't anyone ever told you you were beautiful? They must have!'

'People who loved me,' Cassie mumbled.

'Oh my. And you thought because they loved you . . . but Cassie. You can feel your own face. You must have known you weren't average.'

'You can't feel beauty, Maggie. You can't even sense it. Not the external kind, anyway.'

Maggie forgot herself and nodded silently. 'But you knew Wyatt was handsome,' she remembered suddenly.

'He's too cruel to be ugly,' Cassie responded quickly, and Maggie's musical laughter filled the room.

Helen brought in their first course, and the conversation quickly turned to food, the luxurious appointments of the dining room, and the history of Windrow.

'It's a dreadfully snobbish place, I suppose,' Maggie mused between bites of the fresh, spring salad. 'Harlan Windrow, the founder, started it simply to satisfy the needs of his only son when he was blinded. All the other schools for the blind catered to what he called "the masses", and didn't supply the special education his son needed to take his rightful place in the hierarchy of the American rich.' Maggie's voice was rich with disdain for the long-dead man and his affections. She giggled suddenly. 'Did you know they taught ballroom dancing here in the old days?' she laughed. 'Imagine! For ballroom dancing to be one of the most important things a blind person could learn! Ah, well. It was a different time then, and it toned down a bit after Windrow died. Quite simply, it became a school for the very rich blind; much like other schools, only in addition to the instruction one might get elsewhere, they also taught things like servant management, how to handle reception lines, how to pretend one wasn't blind at all. We've come a long way since then, of course, but Windrow is still very exclusive. It has to be. We're a bit more practical now, but essentially, we still train the very wealthy to cope with blindness in their very special environments. It may sound discriminatory, but it isn't. It's the other schools, in fact, that discriminate against the rich. You can go to any of a hundred schools for the blind in this country and learn how to adjust to a middle-class society and take your place in it; but Windrow is the only school that offers the more well-to-do help in the areas they need it most.'

Cassie's face fell visibly. 'You mean what I'll learn here is only how to be a wealthy blind person? Nothing practical?'

Maggie laughed again. 'That is practical, isn't it? It's the life you came from, and the life to which you'll return. Besides, there would be small point in teaching job skills to the students who come here. I doubt that you'll leave Windrow and start looking for secretarial work. You could pay a secretary's salary for two years on what you paid just to spend three months here. But you know all that.'

You'd be amazed at how much I don't know, Maggie, Cassie thought. And probably more amazed to know that I spent the last dollar I had to get into this place. She tapped her fork idly on the edge of her plate, worry knitting her brows. 'Surely you teach some things even an average person can utilise on the outside?' she asked quietly.

Maggie touched her hand lightly to still the nervous tapping of the fork. 'We teach the blind to be blind,' she said steadily. 'Just like any other school. To be confident, comfortable, and efficient. And we do it in an environment similar to what you left at home. The only thing we omit here is job training. None of our students has much use for that. But as for the rest, you'll find us very thorough, and very demanding.

Now, if you're finished, we should be off for the clinic. The doctors are waiting.'

Cassie nodded silently, placed her napkin carefully on the left side of her plate, and rose stiffly from her chair. 'I'm ready,' she said softly.

Maggie shook her head at the apprehension she saw on Cassie's face, wondering again that with all their advantages, the wealthy could be the most blind of all.

CHAPTER THREE

DR FRANKLIN pulled the complex piece of machinery away from the examination chair in which Cassie sat, flipping up the levers on either side that made it look like a submarine periscope.

'All right, Miss Winters. You can relax now.'

Cassie only realised how rigid her body had been when she tried to lean back. She felt the tug on her arms from hands still tightly clenched around the chair's armrests, and smiled at her own tension. She felt it recede as she concentrated on relaxing her spine.

'Well, Dr Franklin,' she asked with artificial lightness, 'what have you learned?'

The elderly doctor slid a tall stool close to her chair and settled his bulk on to it, folding his arms across the shelf of his stomach. He watched her face carefully. 'I think it would be easier if you told me what you've learned over the years, Cassie. May I call you Cassie?'

'Please do,' she smiled. 'No one called me Miss Winters at home. Except the doorman. It makes me a little uncomfortable. As if I were three or four hundred years old.'

Dr Franklin chuckled. 'Fine. Now tell me what you know about your condition, and I'll fill in the blanks when you're finished.'

She sighed deeply and closed her eyes, then began to recite as if it were a lesson she had memorised long ago. 'I was diagnosed as having hysterical blindness shortly after the accident. My eyes could still see, but my brain refused to accept the signals. The emotional trauma of the accident, it was assumed, and the concussion I suffered, resulted in amnesia—my mind refused to remember something too horrible for it to face, and pulled the curtain in self-defence. It shut out the memory through amnesia, and shut out the world through blindness.' She paused. 'How am I doing so far?'

'Excellent. So far,' he responded. His light eyes narrowed, and a thatch of grey brow met between them. 'Go on.'

Cassie laughed nervously. 'There isn't much more. Except the small catch. The real stickler. As I'm sure you know, hysterical blindness only lasts a few days, or weeks, at most. Then the mind relents, and the patient sees again. And the conclusion is obvious. I've known it for years.' Her long, gossamer lashes fluttered against her cheeks as she struggled for control.

'What conclusion is that, Cassie?' the doctor asked gently.

Her voice was shaky, but decisive. 'My blindness is not hysterical. It never was. If it had been, I would have regained my sight long ago. My blindness is real. It has a physical cause. One they couldn't ascertain years ago, when it happened, or even ten years ago, when I was last examined. But with the advances in technology since, I imagine your equipment can identify the cause easily. That's why your examination was so brief. And you needn't hesitate to tell me about it, Doctor. I accepted a long time ago that my condition was permanent.'

Dr Franklin cleared his throat and leaned forward on his stool to put a large, heavy hand on Cassie's shoulder. 'Let me tell you something about hysterical blindness you may not know,' he began. 'In testing, the eyes still respond to light—even the vast powers of the brain can't stop that involuntary reflex. But they don't respond to visual stimuli, such as an object moving quickly towards the subject's face. There!'

'There what?' Cassie asked, perplexed.

'You flinched!' he said triumphantly.

'What?'

'Concentrate, Cassie. Concentrate on your body. Your head in particular.'

She felt the push of air as his hand rushed towards her face and pulled back suddenly.

'There!' he said again. 'You flinched. Did you feel it?'

'Of course I did,' she answered impatiently. 'You moved something towards my face, and I pulled away. It's a perfectly natural reaction. I *felt* something coming towards me.'

Dr Franklin chuckled. 'Maybe. Probably. But when I tested you on the visual unit, with pictures zooming at you by projector, and no corresponding noise or air motion like my hand made just now, you flinched too. Every time.'

Cassie's eyes narrowed and her throat tightened. 'Meaning?'

'That you can still see, Cassie,' he answered softly. 'You're not blind. You probably never were.'

She tried to swallow the lump in her throat, and pushed the words out between her lips slowly, distinctly. 'Then would you mind telling me, Doctor, why the world has been black for eighteen years?' Her voice rose to a near shriek by the end of the sentence.

His voice was soothing, almost syrupy. 'Think of it this way. The world hasn't been black; your mind has.'

She shook her head violently. 'I don't understand.'

He laughed gently. 'Neither do we. There's a great deal about the brain we'll never understand ... at least not in our lifetimes. You were right about hysterical blindness. It's a pretence the mind can't keep up for long. Yours ended, probably a few days, a few weeks after the accident; we'll never know when for certain; and your brain started receiving the pictures your eyes sent it, just as it should have. It couldn't help it. But it didn't want to, and so it turned away. As if it took the images and hid them immediately in a scrapbook, refusing to look at them. Do you understand? I've never encountered a case quite like it in my own experience, but I imagine there are some documented somewhere.'

Once she started trembling, she couldn't stop, and when the tears finally came, they released the dull, sick ache that had been with her for years, and flowed endlessly.

There was a quiet dignity in the way she sobbed, the doctor thought as he held her gently until the moment passed. 'You really believed it all these years,' he said finally. 'That you were physiologically blind—permanently?'

She nodded against his chest, then pushed herself away. Her eyes were rimmed with red, her cheeks streaked with the paths of persistent tears. 'And now I think this is worse,' she whispered. 'I feel like a charlatan—a fake. All these years, I haven't been blind, but I couldn't see!' Her voice trailed away in another spasm of sobbing and he had to wait until she regained control before he could speak.

'Blind is blind, Cassie; and it's very real, whether it's created by the illusions of the mind or the impairment of the eyes. At least this way there's a chance, a good chance, that you might see again. All you have to do is open the door your mind closed years ago, and that may be the hardest part. Obviously your brain believes whatever is behind that door is far worse than life in the dark. But that's Dr Field's department.'

Her lower lip quivered and she blinked bright tears from the corners of her eyes. He looked at her face carefully, then nodded in satisfaction. 'Come with me, Cassie,' he said gently, and led her from the chair to a low, comfortable couch near the door. 'You sit here for a moment. Juxt relax. I'll report what we've learned to Dr Field, and he'll come to collect you shortly.'

To collect her. Like a bag of garbage. 'Doctor?'

'Yes?'

She caught her lower lip between her teeth and took a deep breath. 'I feel . . . a little like a . . . I'm sorry. I just don't know quite how to explain it. As if I'd been walking around in a cast for eighteen years and just found out my leg wasn't broken after all. I'm not sure which is worse: knowing I don't really need the cast; or admitting I never needed it. Am I making any sense?'

'Perfect sense,' he said kindly.

'It would help, maybe, if I knew it weren't so . . . unusual.'

'I'll be doing a lot of research in the next few days, Cassie. I'll let Dr Field know if . . . when I find a similar case. He'll tell you. And Cassie . . .'

'Yes?'

'You look much too glum for a blind woman who's just learned she has a chance to see again. Cheer up. We're just beginning.'

She gave the kindly doctor a small smile that cracked and disappeared the moment the door closed behind him. She was thinking of another door—the door her mind had closed nearly twenty years before—and wondering fearfully what horrors lay behind it.

'So that's it in a nutshell, Wyatt. I've never seen anything like it.' Dr Franklin leaned back in the groove his body had made in the huge leather chair over the last eight years, and shook his head in bafflement.

Wyatt stood quietly erect in front of the older doctor's desk, his eyes focused on a distant point beyond the bay window. 'You're sure she's not faking,' he said tonelessly; not really as a question, but more as a confirmation of all he had just heard.

'Oh Wyatt! Really!' Dr Franklin snapped, eyeing the younger man with disapproval. 'I don't think I've ever known such a sceptic. It amazes me that you have the success you do with such a cynical attitude. How do your patients ever survive you?'

Wyatt's smile was thin as he dropped his eyes to meet Franklin's. 'Maybe my patients succeed because I'm a cynic; not in spite of it. There are enough of you tea-and-sympathy compassionates around here. You make it too pleasant to be blind. I'm the one who makes it unpleasant, remember?'

Franklin shook his head in dismay. 'I know the philosophy, Wyatt. You don't have to lecture me. I just hate turning the innocents over to you, that's all. They walk out of my office and straight into two weeks of hell with you. No, no; don't say it. I know it already. The humiliation, the degradation, the unforgiving discipline you practice is necessary. What's worse, it works. Makes them strong, independent, confident.' He put his hands into a steeple of fingers and watched absently as he moved them back and forth. 'I'm just afraid that one of these days we'll get a student without the courage to get through it. One who's been so protected, so sheltered, that instead of fighting you and conquering their fears, they'll just crumble instead. And I'm afraid Cassie Winters might be that student.'

'She's stronger than you think she is. They all are.'

Franklin dropped his hands and appraised the young man before him, searching, as he always did, for a hint of emotion concealed behind the strong, even features. As usual, he saw none.

He had grown to love Wyatt over the eight years they had worked together, and thought of him in the same way he would have thought of a son, had he been so blessed. He had even gone so far as to hope his own daughter would somehow lure the young, enigmatic doctor into the family circle, so he would be his son in fact, as well as in thought. But Marianne had strayed as far from the medical field as she could get, eventually marrying an oil rigger who spent three months out of every four stranded somewhere in the Atlantic on a drilling rig, sending home buckets of money and no grandchildren. 'Wyatt Field is the coldest man I've ever met, Daddy,' she had told him after meeting him for the first time. 'I can't imagine how you've grown so fond of him.' Franklin had wondered that himself occasionally. There had never been the slightest display of affection between the two men. Not visibly, at least. But through their joint efforts, many Windrow graduates had gone on to settle comfortably in their darkened worlds, and the mutual achievement of the two doctors had fostered a warm, professional bond of respect that thrived without physical or verbal expression.

'Matt.'

He studied Wyatt's face thoughtfully, marvelling that any man so striking remained relatively aloof from the many attempted persuasions of the women around him. 'He's absolutely the most beautiful man I've ever seen,' his wife Katy had remarked after meeting him years ago. 'Like a Greek god, Matthew; and I'm telling you, if you weren't so damn sexy yourself I'd beg him to run away with me.' She had patted his ever-expanding belly at that point, and had led him like a child to their bedroom. Dear Katy. His dream-woman. Still the same after thirty-seven years.

'Matt.'

He started to attention, then smiled sheepishly. 'Sorry, Wyatt. My mind was busy.'

'It always is. Well, is there anything else I should know about the sacrificial lamb?'

'A lot more, I would think. But her personal history is almost blank, I'm afraid. She's invoked patient privilege with the psychiatrist that treated her ten years ago, so he can't release anything. He did confide to me on the phone that there was little he had learned, anyway. He thinks of Miss Winters as his most resounding failure.'

'Who was it?'

'VanDeMeir.'

Wyatt raised his brows.

'Don't start, Wyatt. He's the best there is in New York City, and you know it.'

'At $400.00 an hour, he ought to be.'

'Five hundred.'

Wyatt shook his head disdainfully.

'Looks to me like the pot's calling the kettle black, Wyatt. If you break down the tuition we charge here, you're not much cheaper.'

The young doctor's lips compressed into a thin line.

'Smooth your hackles,' Dr Franklin chuckled. 'It was just a friendly stab. I know you don't set the rates here. And I know about your charity cases too, in spite of your diligent efforts to hide them. It's the only thing that convinced me you weren't a monster these past eight years.'

Field looked blankly innocent, and Dr Franklin dismissed the pretence with a wave of his hand. 'Don't try to tell me Martin Hausmeyer paid his own way here,' he scolded. 'Gradeschool teachers don't make enough to finance a term at Windrow.'

'What makes you think I helped him?' Wyatt demanded.

Franklin smiled. 'Ever since you joined the staff here, we've had at least two students a year who wouldn't be able to pay their way through a single semester at City College. Somebody was financing them. We all knew it; we just didn't know who. Hausmeyer finally solved the mystery. He told me.'

Wyatt's face darkened with suppressed anger.

'Don't blame him, Wyatt. It was your fault anyway. He's a man of integrity; a proud man. He wanted to pay you back, and you wouldn't let him. He had to take someone into his confidence. He's signed over half interest to every asset he has to you; just in case he should die before he can pay the debt, he said. He wanted someone who knew you to be aware of it.'

The muscle in Wyatt's cheek jumped. 'That's ridiculous. Hausmeyer is a young man. Besides, what would I do with money?'

'Hausmeyer was covering all the eventualities. He wanted his debt paid in case of an unforeseen accident. And it didn't matter that you were too wealthy to miss that money. To him, it was still a debt, and you'll see it paid. I'm certain of that. There's no shame in helping people less fortunate, Wyatt. I don't know why you're so intent on hiding it.'

'Who knows this besides you?'

'No one. And don't ask for my promise. You have it already.'

He expected a muttered oath, but Wyatt relaxed slightly and merely smiled. 'It's time for me to get to work, Matt,' he said, ending the conversation. 'Let me know if you dig up anything on a case similar to the Winters girl, will you? And give my best to Katy.'

'Don't forget dinner Friday, Wyatt.'

'I won't.' He moved to the door of the office then paused, half-turning to face the older doctor. 'Thanks,' he said simply.

Franklin smiled fondly at Wyatt's back as he left the office, anticipating the pleasure of keeping him away from his work for one entire evening; the satisfaction of watching him fill up on Katy's cooking. The boy worked too hard. It was the only thing he ever thought of. Franklin wondered again, as he had hundreds of times before, what dark forces drove the man.

Cassie heard the door click open, and knew immediately through a dozen different sensory receptions that Wyatt Field had come to 'collect' her.

'Hello Dr Field,' she said quietly, wondering if her face still bore the ravages of her earlier emotional release.

'Miss Winters,' he acknowledged brusquely. 'Come with me, please.'

She rose obediently and stood where she was, waiting for him to come and take her arm. He said nothing, and made no move towards her, and she remembered her trip up the stairs with burning humiliation, realising there would be no help from this man—not ever. She turned slowly and edged along the couch to where the sound of his voice had originated, and stopped when she sensed his body before her. She approximated mentally where his eyes would be and looked up, even though she saw nothing.

'Where are we going?'

'For a walk. Out the front door of the clinic—just retrace the way you came in . . .'

'I wasn't paying attention to the way I came in!' she snapped. 'Maggie brought me.'

'. . . and then across the yard to the central fountain,

then straight left, due west, about half a mile. There's a creek there; you'll be able to hear it when you get close enough; with a bench around the base of an old oak tree. We'll sit there and have a talk. The first of many.'

'Sounds perfectly idyllic,' she said sarcastically. 'What a way to spend a summer afternoon.'

'That's what I thought too. Lead on.'

Cassie's mouth dropped open. 'Lead on? Be serious!'

'I'm always serious, Miss Winters. Always.'

She spun away from him and crossed her arms in front of her. 'Forget it. I'm not about to go stumbling around outdoors to satisfy your perverted sadism. You want to sit by a creek all afternoon? Fine. Lead the way. Or go alone.'

His hands were on her shoulders almost before she had finished speaking, and he spun her in place like a top until she faced him once again.

'This is not a contest of wills, Miss Winters. Not one of your high society social games, where you play coy, hard-to-get, or spoiled brat.'

She stood with her mouth foolishly open; sightless, brilliant blue eyes wide in amazement.

'There is no contest here,' he continued in an even voice. 'For the next two weeks, my will is not only supreme, it's inviolate. You'll do what I say, when I say, and I won't waste your money or my time tiptoeing around your delicate sensibilities. Is that understood?'

She swallowed once, hard, then straightened and lifted her chin. 'Dr Field, I've decided not to continue at Windrow. You'll have to find alternate entertainment for the next two weeks. I'll be leaving this evening.'

'Really,' he mocked her.

She nodded once, grateful for the first time in nearly twenty years that she couldn't see the expression on someone's face.

He shifted his weight to stand evenly on both feet, and clenched his face muscles to contain the furious ball of frustration. 'You think because you've learned your blindness isn't physical, that you can cure it yourself, is that it? And that there's small purpose in learning to be an independent blind person if you're going to regain your sight. Am I right?'

'Something like that,' she replied haughtily.

He tightened his fingers on her shoulders until she winced under the pressure. 'Well, let me remind you, Miss Winters, that you've had eighteen years to cure yourself, and you haven't done very well, have you? Just what do you intend to do? Go home, sit back in that Park Avenue tomb you've created, and allow yourself to be babied and pampered and protected until there's no Cassie Winters left? And you think in that kind of environment, growing stagnant and wasted and totally useless, that your sight will miraculously return?' He began to shake her by the shoulders and she had to stiffen her neck to keep her head from bobbing.

'Well it won't work!' he hissed. 'It's what's kept you the way you are!'

He pushed her away roughly and dropped his hands. She took a quick step backward, astounded by the vehemence of his voice and his actions, shaken by the possible truth of what he had said.

'I don't understand you people!' he spat contemptuously, and Cassie was strangely reminded of Helen. 'Content in your gilded cages, all of you! I would think you'd want to be free, but it's terrifying, isn't it? To be responsible for your own life, your own actions; it just scares the hell out of you. Well, I see through you, Miss Winters. It's not that you don't think you need Windrow anymore; you're afraid of what we might accomplish. We just might uncover the demon that's kept you blind, and you can't risk that, can you? You can't face the responsibility of sight. It's too safe, too comfortable—being rich, and being blind.'

Only shock kept Cassie from bursting into tears. She trembled as she stood, but allowed a numbness to spread throughout her body and her mind, insulating her from the harshness of his judgment; from the emotional response that fought to release itself in an

agonised, frustrated scream. She wanted to tell him
there was no estate, no money, no bright, protected
financial future. That there would be no servants, no
luxury, no pampered life ahead, and no Park Avenue
penthouse after the year's lease was up in six months.
But there was a certain prideful satisfaction in holding
it in; in allowing him to think she was just another of
the coddled rich. It seemed like the only edge she had.
To have one secret, just one, from the cruel, hard man
who would probe every other facet of her life within the
next two weeks—that was her only protection. For she
knew now that she needed Window, and needed this
man. He was the only chance she had to regain her
sight; and the only chance she had if she didn't. For the
first time in all of the black years, Cassie acknowledged
to herself that it was time she learned to be blind; long
past time.

She took a deep breath and closed her eyes, finding
an odd sort of peace in the gesture, even though the
world was as dark with eyes open as it was with them
closed.

'If you'll move out of the way, Dr Field, I'll attempt
to find the exit to this building,' she said quietly. 'I'll
also attempt to find the creek, and if I manage by some
miracle to get even close, I ask only that you try to
prevent me from falling in.'

He looked down at her face in quiet amazement.
He hadn't realised until the moment she accepted the
challenge how important it had been to him. The
intensity of his emotion had surprised even him, and
Wyatt Field was rarely surprised by anyone's emotions, least of all his own. He thought he had lost
her; that this would be his first failure; and then
remarkably,   she   had   done   a   complete   turn-
around—forfeited the pampered good life for the
agony Windrow promised. Relief washed over him in
a giddy wave, and he closed his eyes tightly to keep it
inside—where it belonged. He worried briefly that
losing her had been so important, then shrugged it

away as a simple refusal to accept failure. He had never been any good at that.

He stepped to one side and looked at Cassie Winters in profile, respecting the determination behind the fragile beauty of her delicate features. 'Lead on, Miss Winters,' he said quietly. 'I'm right behind you.'

The hollow sound of her footsteps indicated that the clinic hallway was wide and unobstructed. The amplification of the sound told her when she had reached an intersecting corridor, and she turned right automatically, comfortable with the choice. Her brain had recorded the way in and out of the building, she realised. All she had to do was relax and allow it to remember. Her steps were slow and halting, and she had to fight to keep her hands extended from bent elbows as Maggie had taught her, when she instinctively wanted to raise them to wave before her head, as if they could replace her eyes only if they were at eye-level.

'We always protect our heads, our faces,' he commented as he followed a half-step behind and to her left. 'It's pure instinct; to shield the eyes.'

So he noticed her struggle to keep her hands down, and was helping her excuse the errant instinct. Was it that obvious?

'The irony is that the blind have no eyes to protect, and suffer most of their injuries on their legs. But instinct can be blind, too. We have to teach you to fight it off.'

She stepped on the rubber mat at the front entrance and heard the sliding doors whoosh open before her, and at that moment she thought her knees would buckle, letting her crumple to the ground. She stopped dead and tried to control the violent trembling in her legs. She bit down on her lower lip and fought back the tears.

'It's all right,' his voice encouraged her. 'The doors will stay open. You can walk through.'

But it wasn't that. It wasn't that at all. She had just found her way through a strange building on her own.

No guiding hand on her elbow, no words of direction. Nothing. Just Cassie Winters and her senses, operating on her own, relying on no one. And she had made it. The accomplishment was overwhelming, the victory so sweet, and it was all hers. It was nothing to Field. She knew that. But it was her beginning, and the doors that opened before her were opening on a new life. She was exhilarated; and she was terrified; but she walked through the doors silently, holding it all inside.

CHAPTER FOUR

HER confidence evaporated once she stepped outside the building, and she fell prey to a common fear of the blind: the fear of open places. Without walls to touch, to bounce back sounds, there are no points of reference, and Cassie became immediately disorientated. She froze just outside the door, just as she had when the hired chauffeur had dropped her off earlier, and Wyatt knew she would not move again without direction. Whatever her successful walk through the clinic had gained her in confidence was instantly shattered, and experience told him she was once again losing ground to hopelessness.

'Some caution is sensible,' he said quickly, moving up to stand beside her. 'Outside, in particular. There are tricycles, lawnmowers, garden rakes, and other similar death traps lying in wait everywhere in the world.'

She laughed nervously.

'Outside you will almost always need direction. There's no shame in that,' he continued. 'Just walk slowly. We're testing your sense of direction now; not your ability to sense impossible obstacles. That comes later. I'll warn you if you're in danger of running into a tree. Trust me.'

'I think you said that once before,' she remarked drily.

'And I'll say it again. Over and over. It's the most important thing the blind ever learn—and the hardest. To trust a cane, or a guide dog; their own senses, or another person who's trying to help. You will never have confidence without that trust. Now start walking.'

'I'm not really dressed for a walk through the fields,' she said in a small voice, stalling for the first time.

His eyes flickered briefly up and down the slim lines of her blue linen suit, noting with mild amusement the high ruffled collar of the silk blouse, the full cut of the long jacket. Whoever took care of this woman at home had obviously done so for years, and still thought of her as a young girl. Her clothes were almost childishly demure, concealing every line of the body beneath.

'There are no fields where we're going,' he answered impatiently. 'Windrow has five acres of lawn; closely clipped, and immaculately kept. You won't fall into any gopher holes, or stumble into brambles. But it's a warm afternoon. You might want to leave your jacket behind.'

Her hands reached instinctively for the lapels of her suit coat, and she pulled it around her more closely. He had expected that. Even clothes were a part of the defensive syndrome of the blind. The more layers between them and the unknowns of the world, the more secure they felt.

She took a deep, shaky breath, and began to move hesitantly down the steps and towards the sound of the fountain.

After what seemed like miles, but in reality had only been a hundred steps, Cassie was close enough to feel an occasional droplet splash against her face, and her lips lifted in a satisfied smile. She moved closer and closer to the merry sound of splashing water until her foot snugged against the circular concrete base of the pool, then she searched with her hands for the lip of the fountain. It was higher than she had guessed, and she could reach over the side and splash both hands in the cool water without bending. She tipped her head up and let the mist splatter on her face, and laughed out loud.

Wyatt smiled in spite of himself. 'Are you a swimmer?' he asked.

'I used to be. As a child,' she answered distractedly. 'Not for years.'

'You will be soon. That comes next week; when you trust me a little more.'

She raised her head in alarm, the smile fading from her face.

'Don't look so concerned,' he chuckled. 'I promise not to throw you in the creek today.'

She blinked sceptically, then turned left, to face what she hoped would be due west. They didn't speak as she made her way with agonising slowness across the broad lawns. She needed complete silence to concentrate on her first trip across virgin territory, and her ears strained to catch every sound, locating low shrubs by the rustle of their foliage in the light breeze; sensing the closeness of trees by the flutters of birds overhead, the scratching of branches as they rubbed together above her.

The ground inclined downward slightly, becoming spongier under her feet, and she heard the sloshing ripple of water over stones long before Wyatt did.

'What a lovely sound,' she whispered, pausing to listen.

'What sound?'

'The creek, of course.'

Sunlight laced through the leaves of an overhanging branch and speckled her face in a kaleidoscope of dancing light. Her lips parted and turned up slightly at the corners as she listened, and a serenity he had never felt himself glowed on her face. He cleared his throat noisily. 'You take longer steps with your left foot than your right. Remember that. It makes you veer to the left. You'll have to compensate to find the bench I told you about. It's in a straight line from the fountain.'

The serenity vanished and her features hardened with determination as she began to move at a slight angle to the right. The water sounds became louder, and Wyatt watched her carefully as she drew closer and closer to the bank. She stopped suddenly.

'The oak is right there,' she pointed. 'I don't know how far the bench extends from the trunk, and I'd just as soon not crack my shins.'

His brows lifted in surprise. 'How did you know this was the oak?'

She wrinkled her nose delicately. 'It's the only oak

we've come near so far, and if I walk any further, I'll be
in the water.'

'You can *smell* an oak tree?'

'My father's hobby was horticulture.'

'I see.'

'Well?' she asked with a slight edge to her voice.

'Well what?'

'Aren't you going to help me to the bench?'

'Certainly not.'

'Damn you!' She stamped her foot, but the gesture
lost its effect in the soft turf. She spun away from him,
her hair following in a swirling, pale pinwheel, then
kicked off both her shoes with a violence that sent them
spinning end over end through the air in front of her.
She plunked unceremoniously down on the grass.

'You kicked off your shoes,' he said with a thin smile
she could hear in his voice.

'So what!' she snapped over her shoulder, leaning
back on her hands in a childishly defiant posture.

'So you're going to have a hard time finding them,
that's what.'

She compressed her lips and squeezed her eyes shut in
frustration, doing a rapid mental count to ten. The
worst of it was that she had realised her mistake almost
instantly. There was no Mrs Carmody to pick up after
her here. Even the simple pleasure of kicking off her
shoes was to be denied. She made it all the way to
thirty-seven before she trusted herself to speak.

'I'll find them,' she said evenly. 'Myself.'

'Indeed you will.' His smile was almost tender as he
looked down on her stubborn profile, but the
tenderness didn't cross over into his voice. 'We do see
an occasional snake at Windrow,' he said casually.

She jumped to her feet instantly, her eyes wide,
cocking her head as if she could hear the slithering
whisper of dry scales on the grass. She heard his low
chuckle and spun to face it, her lips set in a thin, angry
line.

'All right!' she shouted. 'I'll find the damn bench!'

She moved towards the tree trunk on her knees, her hands extended until they rapped against the solid, even edge of redwood. She put a scraped knuckle to her mouth with a frown, then pulled herself up to sit on the sanded slats that circled the base of the oak.

Wyatt smiled in satisfaction and moved to sit next to her. He leaned back against the broad trunk with a contented sigh, stretched his long legs out in front of him, and turned his head to watch her face.

'My nylons are ruined,' she muttered, fingering the snags on her knees.

'You can afford it,' he said simply.

'I cannot . . .' she started to explain in dismay, then caught herself. 'No one can afford waste.'

'Then walk next time, instead of crawling around on your knees,' he retorted.

She banged a tiny hand down flat on the bench between them, taking satisfaction from the loud crack of sound, pleased at the smarting tingle on her palm.

His laugh was warm and mellow, a sound she would have enjoyed had she been less angry.

'I suppose you're used to being hated,' she spat.

'I am.'

'And it doesn't bother you in the least.'

'Not at all.'

She turned her head to face him, and remained silent for several seconds. Her eyes remained steadily fixed on his, and though he knew it was only coincidence that her gaze seemed to rest directly on his eyes, he felt an uncomfortable sensation of being examined, as if she could see. He studied her face in turn, committing every detail to memory. It was part of his job, he reminded himself. To become so totally familiar with every nuance of expression the face revealed that he could anticipate the thoughts of his students before they realised they had revealed them.

She was so incredibly perfect he felt the childish impulse to reach out and touch her; to assure himself she was real. Her heart-shaped face widened at the high brows arched over large, intelligent eyes. The blue was a uniform, unchanging crystal; the same colour as the lagoons pictured in travel posters of the Caribbean. A delicate blush flowed smoothly over prominent cheekbones to touch a perfectly formed nose with dainty nostrils that flared quickly when she was angry, and pinched slightly when she was frustrated. Her lips rode full and sensuous on a gently rounded chin, and were remarkably expressive; curving to a subtle Mona Lisa smile, thinning to an angry line, or puckering into a childish pout that twisted a tight knot in his chest. Already he had noted these things; filed them carefully away in a mind that would use them later as signposts guiding his own reactions. He continued to tell himself it was only a part of his job, to study the patient so meticulously; yet he had never met a woman he wanted to touch so badly.

'What are you doing?' she asked finally, suspicious at his silence.

'Looking at your face,' he answered honestly.

Her eyes narrowed a fraction of an inch. 'What do I look like?'

'You tell me.'

She shook her head once, and her hair flew back over her shoulder. 'No. I don't want to play psychiatrist. I want to know what *you* think I look like.'

He laughed easily. 'You're paying a great deal of money to "play psychiatrist", as you call it.'

She turned her face away for a moment, pursing her lips, then turned back to him suddenly. 'May I touch you?' she asked.

'Of course.' It was a common enough request. His patients were always intensely curious about him, and he was used to the perpetual flutter of fingers about his face.

Cassie rose to kneel on the hard redwood slats, facing him fully, and he twisted slightly sideways to give her easier access, noting her fruitless efforts to cushion her knees with her skirt.

'Doesn't that hurt your knees?' he asked.

'That's a strange question from a man who's been eagerly waiting for me to fall flat on my face all day.'

He smiled until her hands touched his chest, then composed his face quickly into a rigid mask that would reflect nothing. Her hands moved up to rest on either side of his face, then remained still. He stopped the puzzled frown before it reached his brow. This was totally unlike the rapid flutter of her earlier cursory examination in front of Maggie, and the difference made him immediately uncomfortable.

Her fingers began to move slowly, almost languorously, in cool, smooth circles across his brow, down his temples, her thumbs tracing either side of his nose, pausing further to flick back and forth against the stubble of beard that was already darkening his chin. Her eyes remained wide open and steadily on his face, which was disconcerting in itself, as if the feather-light touch of her hands weren't enough. Normally his patients kept their eyes closed during this procedure, in an instinctive focusing of all their sensory perception to their fingertips. He wasn't used to even the pretence of being visually examined—not by a blind person.

He flicked nervously at his lips with his tongue just as her fingers wandered to his mouth, and she giggled at the physical sensation. She could feel the heat rush to his face, and hesitated before tracing the outline of his lips with one finger. His eyes remained riveted on her face, which reflected only wondering concentration, as she followed the pattern of his mouth with first one finger, then another, then all of them at once. She caught the fullness of his lower lip with a curious pressure of one thumb, and Wyatt suddenly felt the intense heat of the afternoon, and the irrepressible need to draw in more air. His lips parted as he sucked in a deep breath, and Cassie felt the soft, smooth tissue on the inside of his lip with the edge of her thumb, and her own lips parted in an automatic response. Wyatt stiffened immediately, unable to tear his eyes from the soft lips parting inches away from his own, inexplicably moved by an examination he had experienced hundreds of times, hard put to keep his own hands clenched into tight fists at his sides. Her touch was incredibly sensuous; her innocence obviously total. She had no idea of the response she was awakening in him.

Her hands slipped down to circle his neck, then moved across his shoulders, sliding to press gently around the biceps, cupping his elbows, then dropping to hands he opened quickly before she could feel the tightened fists. He shivered as her fingers traced lightly across his open palms, then went immediately rigid when her hands dropped to rest on his thighs.

'What's the matter?' she asked innocently as she felt him tense.

He licked his lips and tried to keep his voice steady. 'Nothing. I've never had such a thorough examination, that's all.'

'What do you mean? Surely you're used to this sort of thing by now?'

He quelled the impulse to clear his throat. 'Patients usually limit their inspection to my face ... sometimes my arms.'

'That's ridiculous,' she said casually, moving her hands around the tight muscles of his thighs. 'You have a body, too. Not just a face and arms. How did they ever know what you looked like?'

He felt a cramp developing in his left thigh, and struggled to relax the muscle under her hand, and failed. His throat constricted, then opened as her hands continued over his knees, down his calves to his feet. There, much to his relief, she pulled her hands away and laughed out loud, sitting back on her heels.

'What's so funny?' he asked sharply, strangely on the defensive.

'There's just something preposterous about a psychiatrist in tennis shoes, that's all,' she laughed. 'Somehow it doesn't fit the image.'

Wyatt felt uncomfortably like he was losing control

of the situation, and responded with irritation out of all proportion to her remark. 'And just what is your image of psychiatrists?' he demanded.

Her hands flew to his face and he jerked his head back in surprise, bumping it sharply against the trunk of the tree. 'What are you doing?' he asked angrily.

'Trying to feel what you look like when you're mad,' she responded calmly, pulling his head gently towards her, unconsciously reaching around the back with one hand to rub the spot where he had bumped it. 'Sorry about your head, by the way.'

Her face was within three inches of his, and he could feel the warmth of her breath against his cheek, and suddenly it was too much. He grabbed at her hands, pulling them sharply away from his face, his own hands quaking as they tightened around hers. Her face immediately reflected dismay, and he gritted his teeth against the image of her wounded eyes, her startled expression. Then without planning, without even realising what he was doing, he released one hand and reached for the back of her neck, pulling her sharply against his chest, covering her parted lips with his, pressing harder and harder, trying vainly to smother the violent throbbing within himself. Her head pulled back against the unyielding pressure of his hand at first, then her lips moved slightly under his, hesitantly, as if she were testing an unfamiliar sensation. He gasped involuntarily at the moist motion beneath his mouth, and tore his lips from hers with a violent twist of his head. He listened to the hoarse, urgent sound of his own ragged breathing, and closed his eyes tightly against the realisation of what he had allowed to happen.

'Damn!' he breathed; then louder, 'Damn!'

She pulled away hesitantly, expecting to be jerked back, but he opened his hands and let her go. She rose from the bench, uncertainty tugging at her brow, and stood silently shifting her weight from one foot to the other, waiting for whatever would happen next.

And what happens next? she asked herself. Simple. In books, this is when he tells you he loves you, and can't live without you. Then you get married and live happily ever after; and somewhere in there, you acquire two children, a dog, and a house in the suburbs. That's what happens when a man kisses a woman like that. In the books, that's what always happens. And let's face it, Cassie, the books are all you have to go by, and this must be that magical thing, love at first sight. Only how can you fall in love at first sight when you can't even see? And that burning flash of heat when he kissed you—is that really love? Is that what it feels like?

Okay, Cassie, she commanded herself silently. How do you handle this? Pretend you have experience. Pretend you're a normal, twenty-five-year-old woman. Pretend you've dated; you've had relationships; you've been kissed a hundred, no, a thousand times. And you know men. You know how their minds work. So what do you do now?

She heard the movements of his slacks scraping against the redwood bench, but didn't realise he had straightened and was staring at her as if she were an enemy he was duty-bound to battle.

When he finally spoke, his voice was caustic and brittle, and that wasn't part of her scenario. 'Sit down, Miss Winters.'

Miss Winters. He called her Miss Winters. Shouldn't he call her Cassie? When you're going to marry someone and live happily ever after, don't you call them by their first name?

She hesitated, then sat next to him cautiously, feeling her way with her hands, keeping her face averted.

He saw her confusion, and fought the fury rising from somewhere deep within himself. It was the first time in his professional life that he had lost control, and he realised bitterly how seriously he may have jeopardised the tenuous doctor–patient relationship. 'What are you thinking?' he asked, trying to sound professional and detached.

Her hands fluttered in her lap in a gesture of frustration. 'Just what you might expect,' she said tremulously.

'That's a trick answer.'

'It was a trick question.'

He smiled a little, pleasantly challenged by her quickness, unpleasantly frustrated by the door she was effectively closing against him. There could be no emotional involvement between them. None whatsoever. Emotionally involved patients become wary, and secretive, and project all sorts of barriers to protect their feelings. 'All right then. I'll be more specific. What do you think of *me*, Miss Winters?'

She pulled in a deep breath, held it in for as long as she could, then exploded with its release. 'I don't know what to think of you! How do you expect me to answer that? First you're arrogant, and insulting, and sadistic, and then . . .' her voice faded to a whisper, '. . . and then you kiss me like that . . .' She shrugged helplessly, and caught her lower lip beneath her teeth.

'I'm sorry if I confused you,' he said gently. 'I didn't mean to do that. My function here is to build your confidence; not break it down.'

Cassie coloured immediately, the bright red of embarrassment diffusing across her face, down her neck, until even her arms felt hot.

So that's what it is, she thought bitterly. Part of the treatment. Kiss the blind girls; make them feel desirable, *normal*; build their confidence and delude them into believing they're something special.

She pressed her fists to her eyes and shook her head, too mortified to speak.

'You have to be on your guard with men, Cassandra,' her father's words came back to her. 'You more than other women, because you'll be an object of pity.'

And that had been the sum of her father's sage advice on love and marriage: that men would pity her, and she might mistake that feeling for something else.

How right you were, Father, she thought to his memory. And I nearly fell for it.

She swallowed a vague, bitter feeling of disappointment, and allowed anger to take its place. She didn't know which would be worse: being kissed out of pity, or as part of a psychiatric ploy.

'Well, Miss Winters? Are you ready to go on?'

Listen to that! Are you ready to go on, he asks; just like nothing happened!

'I can hardly wait,' she said bitterly. 'What happens next? Do we move right from kissing into the rape scene, or are there more preliminaries?'

A deep crease appeared between his brows. 'I think you're over-reacting, Miss Winters . . .'

'Of course I am!' she shouted. 'Crazy people *always* over-react! And I am crazy, you know. I'm the girl with twenty-twenty vision who thinks she's blind, remember?'

'That's not quite the way it is,' he said softly, and there was something almost sinister in his tone. 'You're the girl with twenty-twenty vision who *chose* to be blind; who wants to be blind. I'm beginning to think you enjoy it.'

She caught her breath and marvelled at the depth of his cruelty, and gave in to the overwhelming need to strike out, to punish, to hurt.

'May I touch your face again, Dr Field?' she asked calmly, turning towards him.

'Go ahead,' he said, tensing, trying to sort out the chameleon moods of this strange young woman.

The fingers of her left hand found his cheek quickly, and with that hand as both target and diversion, she brought the palm of her right hand crashing against his other cheek with a resounding slap that shattered the stillness of the afternoon and flung his head sideways.

'No one enjoys being blind, Dr Field,' she said quietly, brushing her palms across the front of her skirt as she stood.

His eyes had flown open in surprise at the force of

the unexpected blow, but now narrowed to slits of light within the dark framework of his lashes. He gritted his teeth until his jaw ached, and willed his hands to remain still. He fought for control of his temper through endless, quiet moments, and Cassie finally blinked nervously, a bright, hard knot of fear growing in her stomach. At last his voice broke the silence, and she breathed quickly in relief.

'Don't ever try anything like that again, Miss Winters.' The words were clipped and ominous. 'I have no compunction whatsoever about turning spoiled, rich blind girls over my knee. And there's no one here to spare you that indignity.'

He rose from the bench slowly, his cheek still smarting, as exhausted as he could ever remember being.

She started when she heard him rise, her legs instinctively tense and ready to flee, but he turned away and his footsteps receded in the general direction from which they had come.

'I'll expect you at supper,' he called over his shoulder, his voice already frighteningly far away. 'With your shoes.'

'Wait!' she cried desperately. 'Wait for me!' Her hands fluttered in panic, and she dropped to her knees quickly, scrambling about the lush grass. 'Dr Field!' she called. 'I can't find my shoes!'

She heard his laugh from a long way off, and sat back on her haunches, completely dumbfounded that he would actually leave her there alone. The shock was quickly replaced by a seed of indignant anger that blossomed into hatred. She almost relished the sensation as she felt it build deep within her chest and swell to fill her with resolve. There was a fleeting, confusing memory of the press of his lips against hers, but it faded quickly, like something that had happened years ago, and was barely worth recalling.

She bent her head to the task of finding her shoes, searching the grass with long, methodical sweeps of her hands. At the moment, she felt nothing but a determination to retrieve her shoes and return to her room; a triumph she would fling in the face of Dr Wyatt Field with the same satisfaction she had felt when her palm had connected with the side of his face.

The fear was yet to come.

CHAPTER FIVE

MAGGIE leaned over the porch railing, her fingers beating an unconscious tattoo on the smooth wood, her eyes focused intently across the grounds towards the creek. She breathed a short, exasperated sigh of relief when she saw Wyatt's tall frame come into view, then compressed her lips when she noticed he was alone. Her face darkened as he approached, and she straightened, hands on hips, and glowered down at him from the top of the stairs.

'Where is she?' she demanded.

Wyatt tipped his head up to gaze at the tiny, angry figure, and his lips curved in a tired smile. 'She's out by the creek—looking for the shoes she kicked off in a fit of temper.'

Maggie's eyes widened in disbelief. 'You left her out there alone? Wyatt, what's come over you? You can't do that!'

'It's already done.'

'Well, it's going to be undone. I'm going after her.' Maggie came down the stairs in a flurry of determination, and only the strength of Wyatt's arm prevented her from racing across the road to the rolling lawns that led to the creek.

'Maggie,' he said gently. 'Give her a chance. She's stronger than you think she is; stronger than she thinks she is; and this is her first real test. She'll make it, if you don't ruin it for her. She needs to do this by herself.'

'And what if she falls into the creek?' Maggie asked testily. 'Cracks her head on the rocks, or breaks an arm? What then? You've never left a new student totally alone before. You've at least stayed within watching distance.'

'That won't work with this one. She's too perceptive. She'd know I was there.'

Maggie eyed him doubtfully. 'You're too hard on them, Wyatt. There isn't a trace of compassion in you, and I think this one is going to need it.'

His lips made a contemptuous downward arc. 'You sound like Matt. You think she needs compassion? You dish it out. That's your department, not mine.'

Bright red curls quivered as Maggie shook her head. 'But it's only her first day. Why push her? You've got three months.'

Wyatt pulled her to face him and spoke with an intensity that always made her nervous. 'You're wrong. I've only got two weeks of my own, and that's what I need to get inside her head—time alone with her. Besides, she's different, Maggie. I'm not just teaching this one to be blind. I've got to make her see.'

Maggie frowned up at him. 'Even if it breaks her?'

Wyatt shrugged coldly. 'That's exactly what it's going to take.'

She was about to begin a violent protest, but a warning flicker in his eyes stopped her. She had learned long ago that none of her impassioned pleas for kindness would alter his harsh methods, and he had made it painfully clear that he would not tolerate her interference.

She made a small sound of impotent rebellion, and sat down hard on the porch steps. 'You're a hard man, Wyatt,' she grumbled. 'There's no talking to you; none at all.'

'Kindness doesn't heal all wounds, Maggie,' he said gently, smiling down at her. 'Especially not the big ones. When are you going to learn to trust me?'

She batted at the big hand that ruffled her hair affectionately. 'Ah, leave me be, Wyatt. We'll be fighting over this one for the next two weeks. We might as well take our corners now.'

'Whatever,' he shrugged in amusement, and settled next to her on the stairs.

Maggie looked over at him with a mixture of fondness and exasperation, remembering the not-too-distant past when she thought the sun rose and set behind those cool blue eyes. It was a natural enough mistake, she consoled herself. You'd be a fool not to fall in love on sight with a man who looked like that; and an even bigger fool if you ever took it seriously. He was a loner, that one; with moods as black as a starless night, and a heart buried too deep for touching. She heaved what her mother would have called an Irish sigh, for her mother never believed, until the day she died, that any other nationality ever understood melancholy.

'It may be a long wait, Maggie,' Wyatt said absently, looking across the grounds that sloped down to the creek.

'I've got time,' she said quietly, following his gaze. 'I'm young yet.'

While Maggie and Wyatt waited patiently over a quarter of a mile away, Cassie fumbled helplessly beneath the shade of the ancient oak, still searching for her second shoe. The first had been easy to find, having landed close to where she had kicked it off; and when her hand had finally encountered it, she clutched it to her breast in a gesture of smug triumph. For one brief moment, she felt a twinge of sympathy for the sighted people who would never experience such sweet victory from a task as simple as finding a shoe. But finding the second was proving impossible, and frustration quickly replaced satisfaction as she scrambled about on her hands and knees. She felt her nylons give and tear as twigs and pebbles pressed sharp indentations into her knees.

Her search brought her closer and closer to the bank of the creek, and the sting of unshed tears prickled behind her eyes as she moved her arms in wide, desperate arcs over the close-cropped grass.

'Dammit!' she cursed aloud, and pushed back to sit on her haunches, her throat tight and dry with the prolonged effort not to cry.

It wasn't fair. It simply wasn't fair. What did the almighty Dr Field know about being blind? How dare he leave her out here alone, with the imperial command that she find her own shoes, when he knew perfectly well that it would be impossible!

She struggled to her feet, still clutching the first shoe, and it was only when she swept a wayward strand of light hair from her cheek that she realised how dishevelled she must look. She brushed angrily at the front of her suit, wondering if the gesture would do anything to make her look less like she had been crawling on her hands and knees for the last half hour.

Suddenly the sound of his voice played back in her mind, and she reproached herself for ever thinking it was mellow and rich. It was a hard voice, really; sharp with contempt; and the prospect of facing its owner shoeless became absolutely unacceptable. She dropped back down to her hands and knees with a renewed, furious determination, and began the search again.

She was at the edge of the bank, her left hand skirting its rim while the happy sound of water rushed below her. Her movements were methodically thorough, covering the search pattern she had thought out carefully. She would start at the bank, scouring an area as wide as her arms would reach, then move gradually towards the old oak. The possibility of the soft ground giving way under her weight had never occurred to her, and when it happened, she was totally unprepared. One moment her knees were braced firmly on solid ground; the next moment the ground was gone, and her feet scrambled frantically against the crumbling footing of the steeply sloped bank that dropped to the water below. She gasped in a jolt of surprise, too frightened to scream, clutching desperately to the meagre hold of her hands on the bank's edge above her.

She had no way of knowing how great a drop it was to the creek below; whether the ground's slope gentled and levelled beneath her; or whether the drop-off was straight. And for the moment, assessing such possibilities was beyond her. She knew only that her hands were losing their precarious purchase on the bank's edge; that her feet dangled in mid-air when she stopped driving with them even for an instant; and that she was falling.

The water below mocked her with its jolly gurgle as it rolled over stones in its path, and she tried to guess its distance from her feet by its sound. A foot? Two feet? Five? Far enough to break a leg? Deep enough to drown?

The first tremor of genuine terror started low in her stomach, and travelled up through her body until it climaxed in a slight, defeated whimper that escaped her lips the moment her hands lost their grip. She opened her mouth to a scream, her eyes wide with fear, and then she felt herself begin to drop.

She fell a full three inches to the soft sand that lined the creek bed, and the shock at finding herself so close to solid ground stunned her more than a serious fall would have. She stood perfectly still, her mouth open, recalling the fear, breathing in short, shallow gasps. Then she imagined the picture she must have made, clinging desperately for life to the bank while her feet dangled mere inches from safety, and she began to laugh hysterically, sagging to her knees in the sand, letting the tears fall free in relief.

She cried and she laughed, hugging her shoulders, hunched over her knees, and threaded through the conflicting emotions was a small knot of hatred growing quietly against the man who had caused it all.

Finally she leaned back on her heels, shuddering with the effort of deep, cleansing breaths, and wiped her palms across her tear-stained cheeks. She wanted to swear; to spurt forth an endless string of violent epithets that would burn the very air with their vehemence; every one of them directed towards Dr Wyatt Field. She pressed her lips tightly together against the impulse, then realised with a start that she could say whatever she liked. For the first time in eighteen years, she was out of sight, and out of hearing of any other human being. She was absolutely alone.

The realisation was sobering, and she blinked slowly, considering it. No Mrs Carmody, no Father, no servants; just Cassie. Cassandra Winters, alone in the world. The recklessness of adventure, and the solemn weight of responsibility, fought in a mind that had never experienced either one, and she rose slowly to her feet, feeling that the earth might part and swallow her at any moment.

'This is going to be very hard,' she said aloud in an ominous prediction of her future, and her voice sounded small and uncertain in the open air.

'Well, there you are!' Maggie's cheerful voice penetrated the fog of her busy thoughts, and suddenly Cassie heard the fountain. She was there, then. She had done it. She had found her way up the bank from the creek, found both shoes, and found her way back to the main house. All by herself.

There was a pathetic, ragged dignity in the way she straightened to the sound of Maggie's call, lifting her chin proudly, facing the voice as if it were a heralding bugle proclaiming a victor's return from war. Her lips lifted in a strained smile as she walked towards Maggie, wearing the torn, soiled blue linen like a flag of honour.

'Dear God,' Maggie whispered under her breath, taking in the ragged nylons, the tousled hair, the impossible ruin of the blind girl's suit. 'Well, Wyatt,' she hissed in an aside, 'there's your handiwork! I hope you're satisfied!'

Wyatt's eyes narrowed as he watched Cassie cover the distance between them with short, stiff steps; then he caught the determined set of her jaw; the faint but resolute set of her shoulders. 'I am, Maggie,' he answered softly. 'I am indeed.'

He waited until she was only a foot from him before he spoke, and his voice brought up up sharply. 'I see you found your shoes, Ms Winters.'

The sightless eyes flashed in angry recognition and she turned to face the sound of the taunting voice. 'Of course I did, Doctor,' she said haughtily, barely controlling her temper. 'Nothing to it.'

Maggie noticed the residual tremor of Cassie's hands at her sides, and jerked her head to flash a silent, angry reprimand at Wyatt, but he merely closed his eyes. 'And how was your first walk alone outside?' he asked.

'Infinitely preferable to my first walk with you,' she snapped, and Maggie beamed at the fiery retort.

Wyatt dismissed her hostility with a noisy sigh, and told Maggie with a wink that he was well pleased with his afternoon's work. 'I suggest you clean up before dinner, Ms Winters,' he called over his shoulder as he turned to walk away. 'You're quite a sight as it is.'

'Damn him!' she muttered under her breath, then the warm pressure of Maggie's hand on her arm reminded her of her presence, and she allowed her shoulders to sag in exhaustion.

'Come on, Cassie,' Maggie soothed when Wyatt was out of earshot. 'I'll give you a hand. Whether he likes it or not.'

She guided a sullen, shaken Cassie to her room, knowing she was breaking every house rule to offer this kind of assistance to a patient, and not caring. The girl had obviously been through enough for one day.

Later, as she sat pensively on the bed, waiting for Cassie to finish in the shower, she wondered for the hundredth time at the unrelenting harshness of the man.

Refreshed by the steaming, driving pellets of a hot shower, feeling renewed by the simple act of washing her hair, Cassie emerged from the bath adjoining her room and stood towelling her hair in the centre of the space between bed and dresser. 'Am I keeping you from anything, Maggie?' she asked the silent presence she sensed sitting on the bed.

'No . . . o . . . o . . .'

'What's wrong? Your voice sounds funny.'

Maggie suppressed the smile automatically.

'Nothing's wrong. Nothing at all. Old customs, I suppose. Most of our students are modest to the extreme.'

Cassie's hands stopped in the motions of drying her hair, and she laughed out loud. 'I forgot,' she said sheepishly. 'I'm naked.'

'You certainly are,' Maggie giggled.

Cassie walked hesitantly to the closet and fumbled through the garments until she felt the plush velour of her robe. 'Modesty is a trait you never learn when someone dresses you every day,' she explained, wrapping the pink robe around her. 'It never occurs to you. Especially when you can't see your own body anyway.'

Maggie nodded, smiling. 'Most of the students come here after a sudden blindness. They still harbour all the old taboos of sighted people. We've never had anyone here who's been blind as long as you have.'

Cassie sank disconsolately to the chair in front of the dressing table. 'Or one as helpless,' she sighed. 'I think I'd leave today if it weren't for you, Maggie. The thought of spending two solid weeks with Dr Field makes me want to bolt and run.'

Maggie laughed easily. 'You all sound the same at the beginning, but you'll change your mind about him, Cassie. I promise.'

Cassie stared sightlessly into the distance, flushing as she recalled the kiss that was contrived to 'build her confidence'. 'I think he's a cruel, thoughtless man,' she murmured. 'I don't think I'll ever understand him.'

Maggie slapped her knees and rose from the bed. 'None of us do,' she admitted. 'But fortunately, you don't have to. He's the one who's supposed to understand you. Now. How about the black jumpsuit tonight? I'll bet you're stunning in black.'

Sure, Cassie thought ruefully. See the stunning blind girl. See her trip over chairs and run into walls. Stunned, maybe, But stunning? Not a chance.

'Maggie?' Her voice was timid. 'Is it this hard for everyone?'

Maggie's brows twitched in sympathy at the troubled face turned towards her. 'Hard? So far you've made it look easy,' she answered brightly. 'You made quite a bit of progress for your first day; getting back from the creek on your own.'

Cassie smiled and started to pull a comb through her hair. 'Yes, I did that much, didn't I?' Then she told Maggie about her time at the creek after Dr Field had left her, and in the telling, the remembered fear and frustration faded, and all that remained was a bright sense of accomplishment.

Father would have been proud. Or would he? He had never encouraged her efforts to gain independence. In fact, he had thwarted them all. One by one, every request had been denied ... public school, going to Windrow, and most surprising of all, entering therapy. At the time, she had wondered if his reluctance to have her see a psychiatrist meant that he didn't want her to see again—ever. Maybe he liked her blind, and totally dependent on him. Maybe he was afraid he would lose her if she regained her sight. After all, normal people left home as adults; for careers, marriage, a life of their own. But Cassie stayed with Daddy; right until the end.

She shook away the memory, refusing to believe that anyone could be that selfish. Besides, her father had been right. When she finally defied him openly by spending a year in psychiatric therapy, they both suffered through endless, unanswered questions, and a painful probing of the past ... all for nothing.

'You see, Cassandra?' he had admonished her gently on the day she finally gave up. 'Trying to remember has done nothing but cause us both pain, and we don't really need more of that, do we? Wasn't losing your mother enough?'

She had felt a horrible guilt, then, for opening the wounds of a man who had done nothing but cherish and protect her; and decided that if remembering the accident was the only key to her sight, she would rather be blind.

She pressed her fingertips to her temples, trying to force back the headache that always accompanied thoughts of her father.

'Just as I thought,' Maggie's voice sifted through the fog of her reverie. 'That outfit is gorgeous! Come on. Let's go rattle the evil doctor's cage.'

Cassie forced a smile as Maggie steered her towards the door, feeling very much like a human sacrifice on her way to the lip of a volcano.

Maggie defied Wyatt openly by leading Cassie downstairs and directly to his table in the dining room. She turned her back on his dark frown of disapproval as soon as Cassie was safely seated.

A muscle twitched in Wyatt's cheek as he watched Maggie walk away, and he made a mental note to talk to her later. 'Black suits you,' he said finally, turning his attention to Cassie.

'Does it?' she asked indifferently, distracted by the sounds around her. The dimensions of the dining room seemed to have shrunk with the subdued noises of other diners. Silverware scraped against fine china; low-toned conversations hummed busily; and occasionally fragile crystal rang in clear, silver tones as two glasses were brought together. 'Who are all the other people here?' she asked.

'The rest of the staff. Teachers, nurses, whoever's on duty. We all take the evening meal here. Gives the students some social time alone in the main dining hall, away from our supervision.'

Cassie squirmed in her chair, uncomfortable in the presence of so many strangers. 'Will I meet them?' she asked hesitantly.

'Definitely not,' he answered firmly. 'Not for two weeks, anyway. As far as these people are concerned, you won't exist until I say so.'

'What kind of a stupid rule is that?' she demanded.

'I'll be living here for three months. It's only natural that I should get to know them!'

There was a thin edge of exasperation in his voice. 'Everything we do here serves a purpose, Ms Winters. For the first two weeks, the staff here will represent all the strangers you'll encounter on the outside when you leave. They wouldn't be very effective in that role if you got to know them all. You can't make everyone in the world your friend. There will always be strangers. You have to learn to deal with that.'

Her lower lip rolled petulantly, but she recognised the logic of the argument. Strangers were the unseen, unknown enemy to the blind. In a subconscious effort to eliminate the enemy, she felt an overpowering urge to become acquainted with everyone she encountered, so there would be no strangers left.

'But that's not the only reason, is it?' she asked with sudden insight. 'By enforcing my isolation from other people, you make me more dependent on you, right?'

He smiled at her perception, and her obvious hostility. 'Exactly right,' he admitted. 'For two weeks, at least, I'm all you've got.'

'Except Maggie,' she reminded him.

'Except Maggie . . . provided she doesn't violate any more rules.'

Cassie panicked automatically at the thought of being deprived of Maggie's gentle understanding. Not only was she a safe harbour after Wyatt's demanding intolerance; she also promised to be the closest to a personal friend Cassie had ever had. 'What do you mean? What rules has Maggie violated?'

'She's leading you around like a guide dog. Replacing whomever did that for you at home.'

Restrained by decorum that had been part of her existence for as long as she could remember, Cassie leaned towards the sound of his voice and kept her own quiet and controlled. 'It's my first day here,' she said levelly, 'and it hasn't been very pleasant. Stumbling through a room full of strangers to make it to this table would have been the last straw. Maggie was sympathetic enough to understand that, and helped me. Many strangers on the outside would have been as kind, although I'm sure that the thought would never have occurred to you.'

Wyatt smiled at the colour flooding her cheeks, admiring the control she exercised. He made certain there would be no trace of a smile in his voice when he spoke.

'There is no excuse for what Maggie did, and it will not happen again. From now on, you're on your own, even if it means I have to suspend Maggie for the duration of your stay in the main house. Like it or not, Ms Winters, you're going to learn to be blind.'

The colour fled from her face, leaving two hot spots of red on cheeks otherwise white. 'You love the power you wield in this little kingdom of yours, don't you?' she accused him. 'Well, you're not the only psychiatrist in the world. I'm sure you could be replaced.'

His smile broadened at the empty threat. 'This isn't the outside, Ms Winters. You're in no position to dismiss me, and you'd be a fool to try. I'm the very best there is. Frankly, you're lucky to have me.'

She bit down hard on impotent anger, restraining herself from any visible display. She would tolerate this impossible man, just as she would tolerate the eccentricities of any competent servant. If time proved him incompetent—well, that would be something else. She swallowed her indignation and sat quietly. A sudden shudder passed through her body as she recalled the pressure of his body against hers back at the creek. She fought against the memory, willing it away, and her nostrils flared with the effort.

Wyatt saw the shudder, assumed it was anger, and smiled. He watched emotions flash across her face as she came silently to terms with his absolute authority. Her anger was good. He could use that against her mind, as long as it didn't become too intense. He decided to temper it a little.

'I've taken the liberty of ordering for us, Ms Winters. I hope you don't mind. Our chef prepares squab only occasionally, but it's the best you'll find anywhere. I didn't want you to miss it.'

She inclined her head slightly, tensed in her chair as if she were facing an animal that seemed tame, but one that could turn on her at any moment. She listened to the merry sound of liquid being poured into a glass at her right hand.

'This is a light Chablis,' his voice continued warmly. 'Nothing spectacular, but excellent with the squab.'

The fingers of her right hand crept unobtrusively to her glass, guided by the placement of the silverware, until she found the stem of the heavy, crystal goblet. Wyatt watched the practised manoeuvre with a sardonic lift of one brow while he filled his own glass. It still amazed him that the wealthy blind learned to conduct themselves with the grace of sighted people at the dinner table, long before they ever thought it important to learn to cross the street.

'Shall we toast your future, Ms Winters?'

She shrugged elegantly as his glass touched hers, wondering what Dr Field would think if he knew the future he was toasting was haunted by the bleak prospect of poverty.

'To my future,' she agreed quietly, 'and what you will make of it.'

The wine was indeed excellent, and after her first glass, Cassie began to relax. It was good to sit at a table finely prepared, lulled by the murmurs of contented diners, surrounded by the sounds of a room devoted to elegance and people who appreciated it. The familiar environment was comforting, and it was easy to pretend that this was simply a continuation of life as she had always known it, and not the beginning of the end of the only existence for which her life had prepared her. And it was harmless, she thought. Perfectly harmless. To forget what lay ahead, for just a time; to simply enjoy what she had now. She would face the future when she had no choice. For the moment, she was anticipating an excellent meal with an attractive man in luxurious surroundings, and for the moment, that was enough. She heard wine splashing into her glass for the second time.

'Where do you live, Dr Field?' she asked suddenly, remembering that part of this picture should be casual conversation.

'Just a few miles from here.'

'In a town?'

'No. It's a country house. On the river, in fact.'

Cassie tried to picture the stern, angular darkness she imagined as Dr Wyatt Field in a cottage surrounded by open fields and flower gardens, and nearly laughed out loud. He would be better suited to a castle with a moat. Someplace dark, with no electricity. She kept her thoughts to herself, and said instead, 'I used to live in this area myself, as a child. From what I remember, it was beautiful. Especially in the autumn.'

'It still is. Did you find adjusting to the city difficult?'

She turned sightless eyes in his general direction and smiled. 'Are we going to have a psychiatric session before dinner?'

He laughed gently. 'Think of it as an idle question. Simple curiosity. For this meal at least, we'll forego the doctor–patient relationship. We'll just be two people getting to know one another.'

'Do you really think you can manage that?' she asked without thinking. 'Forgetting our respective roles?'

He frowned at her playful question, thinking of how pleasant it would be to disregard their professional relationship permanently. 'It would be dangerous to forget that entirely,' he said softly, permitting himself that one lapse into sincerity, 'but we can at least put it into the background. Temporarily, of course.'

She nodded slowly, and he found himself fascinated with the shadow her chin made across her neck. 'All right, then,' she said. 'No. Adjusting to the city wasn't as hard as you might think. The country tends to be very boring when you're blind. Not enough noise. Father used to take me to the country on summer weekends for a few years after the accident. When he realised I could hardly wait to get back to the city, the trips stopped. You need eyes to appreciate the country.'

'Some blind people would disagree with you. They find the city intimidating; frightening.'

Her face clouded with memories of the afternoon. 'I can't imagine anything in the city as frightening as my first afternoon here,' she put in quietly. She sensed his discomfort in the sounds of his weight shifting in the chair.

'Let's forget this afternoon,' he said shortly.

She shrugged in pretended nonchalance, wondering which part of the afternoon he wanted her to forget. The kiss, obviously. Just another phase in your treatment, Ms Winters. Nothing noteworthy, and for God's sake, don't take it personally.

'So,' he continued, his voice formal and stiff, 'tell me about your life in the city. How do you fill your time?'

She sighed and leaned back in her chair, remembering. 'I read a lot—braille, of course—and listen to music. Ocasionally Father would take me to the symphony. And I spent a lot of time in the park, just listening.'

'Central Park?'

'Yes. It was right across the street.'

'So you read about other people's lives, eavesdrop on other people's conversations, and listen to music other people make. Fine. What about your own life? What do you do for yourself?'

She bristled at the implication that all her living was done vicariously, stung with the truth of it, and recognised that he had slipped back into his role as psychiatrist. 'For myself,' she snapped, 'I go sightseeing. What did you expect?'

He chuckled at her temper. 'I expected a social life,' he said. 'You don't need eyes for that. What about friends? Lovers?'

'That's an impudent question! And one a gentleman would never ask a lady on their first evening together!'

He sighed with exasperation. 'Let's not carry the pretence too far, Ms Winters. You aren't here for a good time, and this isn't a first date.'

'If it were, there would certainly never be a second!'

His smile was insolent, and knowing. 'So you have no friends to speak of, and certainly no lovers. Amazing, at your age. Sounds like a pretty empty existence to me.'

The colour rushed up from her breast to her face, and Wyatt watched the physical evidence of her embarrassment with inordinate fascination.

'And what about your social life, Dr Field?' she asked cuttingly. 'Who is your woman of the moment?'

He chuckled openly. 'You've decided then, that I'm not married?'

'Obviously not.'

He raised straight, black brows and smiled. He was beginning to enjoy the conversation. 'Why obviously?'

'You're too egotistical to maintain any long-term relationship with a woman; provided you could find one who would have you, which is doubtful.'

'True enough,' he conceded. 'I like living alone. And to answer your question, my personal life is none of your business.'

'But mine is your business?'

'Precisely. That's what you're paying me for.'

Cassie gritted her teeth in frustration. 'It's impossible to pretend for even one meal that you are anything but a doctor, and I am anything but your patient. Even the pretence is foolish. You're obviously incapable of any other type of relationship. So let's drop it. What would you like to know about me, Dr Field, as a psychiatrist?' She tensed in her chair, verbally offering her co-operation, but subconsciously throwing up the barriers against him.

'Nothing for the moment,' he replied easily. 'Helen's bringing our soup.'

Helen served the entire meal with the same, formal

deference of any household servant, but Cassie missed the warm camaraderie she was used to at home. Pampered for years by the unspoken sympathy of the entire household staff, Helen's reserve was a disturbing contrast. 'Please call me Cassie,' she said as Helen served the squab, but the reply had been curt and definite. 'I think not, Ms Winters.' Imagining Helen was merely obeying the rules of non-intimacy which applied to all the staff save Maggie for the first two weeks, Cassie did not take the remark personally; but oddly enough, it seemed to disturb Dr Field. 'That will be all, Helen,' he had said, and disapproval was evident in his voice. Even the starched rustle of Helen's skirt had sounded angry as she left the table, and her footsteps were heavier than usual. Apparently Cassie was not the only one who found Dr Field's manner offensive.

'You were right about the squab,' Cassie admitted reluctantly as her plates were removed. 'It was everything you promised.'

Wyatt poured rich, black coffee from a sterling silver carafe, and allowed himself the luxury of imagining for a moment that Cassie Winters was not blind, and not a patient. It was too easy. Sitting here, showcased by the luxury to which she had been born, her grace and confidence were evident in every gesture. Totally comfortable with the mechanics of eating and drinking, one had to pay strict attention to realise she was blind at all. The clumsy awkwardness of uncertainty was totally absent now, and he was almost mesmerised by the simple pleasure of taking a meal with an extraordinarily beautiful woman.

'What do you really see in your future, Ms Winters?' he asked quietly, watching her expression over the rim of his cup.

'I try not to think about it,' she replied honestly, and the hopelessness of her answer disturbed him.

'Marriage?' he persisted. 'Children?'

She smiled ruefully, and he noticed too acutely the way only one side of her mouth turned up when she was bitterly amused. 'That would seem to be the only alternative for a person like me, wouldn't it? But to tell you the truth, I've never considered it.'

'That's a strange answer. A woman like you must have been forced to consider it by any number of eager young men. Weren't you ever attracted to any of them?'

She blinked slowly, trying to decide how open she had to be, then reminded herself that this man, hateful as he may be, had to know everything about her. She had no time to be coy; no time to be ashamed to admit that for a woman in her mid-twenties, she was painfully without experience. 'There were never any eager young men, Dr Field,' she admitted finally. 'Never a friend, outside the family; and certainly never a lover. You were right about that. I had no opportunity to meet anyone in the life Father structured for me.'

Wyatt bit his lip and frowned, but his voice was steady, and non-committal. 'You'll excuse me if I find that hard to believe,' he said carefully.

'Nevertheless, it happens to be true. I never attended school, and although my tutoring was excellent, it didn't provide much in the way of a social life. And Father seemed to retreat after Mother died; he rarely saw anyone, so there wasn't much stimulation from that quarter either. I met only those people who lived in our building, or people I happened to stumble into at the park—literally. Unfortunately, Prince Charming was not among them, and even if he had been, Mrs Carmody would have been a real deterrent. She was my constant companion, and I suspect she has a rather low opinion of men in general.'

Wyatt's lips pursed in a silent whistle. 'Then you've been totally isolated. All these years.'

Cassie sighed and wondered if it was worth the effort to defend her father. 'Totally protected,' she conceded. 'And I guess that's the same thing from your point of view.'

'So for all practical purposes, I'm the first man you've related to on any but a casual level.' His eyes were dark with anger at the misguided notions of Cassie's dead father, but his voice was deceptively light.

'Related to!' Cassie laughed suddenly. 'Dr Field, you're the first man I've even talked to alone! Except for Father, of course; and the servants.'

'Did you ever resent that?'

She sighed tolerantly, then smiled. 'No Dr Field. I regretted it, of course; but I didn't resent it. And in answer to the question you haven't asked yet, I did not hate my father. I loved him very much.'

He could feel his face darken as the blood of anger flooded his cheeks. 'I don't know a single person who wouldn't rebel against such confinement,' he said carefully.

'Well, now you do.' She looked straight ahead, her eyes steady, and Wyatt could not help but think of an abused child. Loved, spoiled, sheltered; but abused none the less, by deprivation. He struggled to control the unreasoning hatred he was building up against a dead man; struggled to keep the ugly sound of it out of his voice.

'What a waste!' he snapped, losing his age-old battle against his temper, and immediately regretting his lapse.

She raised her eyebrows at the unexpected intensity of his emotions, but he changed the subject quickly. 'More coffee?'

She moved her hand to cover the top of her cup. 'No thank you. But I'd love a walk. That's one luxury I was never permitted in the city—a walk outside after dark. May I do it here?'

'Of course. Blind people make lousy muggers. Walking the grounds here is perfectly safe.'

Wyatt rose and pulled out her chair, then she felt the gentle nudge of his elbow as he offered his arm. She hesitated before taking it. 'I thought guiding the blind was forbidden here.'

'I'm not totally without manners, Ms Winters. You'll have plenty of chances to stumble in and out of this room on your own. Tonight you happen to have an escort, and an escort would offer his arm to any lady, blind or not.'

'Thank you, Dr Field,' she said graciously, and slipped her hand through the crook of his elbow. He tensed slightly at her touch, and she felt the ridge of a taut bicep press down on her fingers. It wasn't like taking her father's arm. It wasn't like that at all.

They walked the circle of the campus in relative silence, broken only when they passed a building Wyatt would identify. 'This is the dormitory,' he said once, 'where you'll live later on. It's coming up on your right, and if you're paying attention, you'll know immediately whenever you come to it.'

'I haven't been paying attention,' she admitted. 'I'm enjoying myself far too much. But a child could find it. The sidewalk changes from cement to brick, right here.' She stopped suddenly. 'I assume that if I turn here, the brick walk will lead right to the door.'

He tightened his arm to press her hand. 'Excellent. There's obviously nothing wrong with your powers of deduction.'

'Are all the buildings identified like this?'

'Yes. This walk is brick, the cafeteria's is pebbled asphalt, the classroom building has a cobblestone walk, and the gymnasium's is simply a dirt path.'

'What about winter?'

'The walks are all heated,' he replied. 'And drained. These are the only guideposts our people have. It wouldn't do to have them obscured by snow.'

'Very clever,' she said.

'Thank you.'

'Your idea?'

'Of course.'

She considered for a moment the irony of a man who seemed so outwardly hostile towards the blind, and so intolerant of their condition; and yet who had obviously put a great deal of thought into making some parts of their stay at Windrow easier. He was a paradox beyond her understanding, and she shrugged lightly, deciding not to try. She breathed deeply of the night air, pulling the unfamiliar scents of the country surroundings into her lungs. 'Now this is luxury,' she sighed. 'Walking outside after dark. May I do it every night?'

He moved forward again as he spoke, and she matched his long stride, delighting in the pull of unused leg muscles. 'Any time you like, if you find the time, that is. The sidewalk circles the campus, so you can't possibly get lost. If you walk long enough, you'll always end up back where you started.'

'And how about the main house? How do I find that?'

'You'll hear it,' he chuckled. 'That was Maggie's contribution. It's the only building with a noisemaker. I'm surprised you haven't noticed it already.'

She slipped her arm further into his and subconsciously walked closer to him.

'Cold?' he asked, looking down at her.

'Just a little. You can almost smell fall around the corner. But of course I'm not wearing a jacket like you . . .' She stopped suddenly and moved to face him. Her hands were on his chest before he had a moment to wonder at her actions. They moved lightly up to his throat, tracing the collar of his shirt, then down over the outline of his tie to the buckle on his belt. They lingered there for a moment, then dropped back to her sides, and he took the first breath he had taken since she touched him. She tipped her head back and smiled.

'I didn't know what you were wearing,' she explained. 'What colour is the shirt?'

'White,' he whispered, still tense from her unexpected inspection.

'And the tie?'

He bent his head to look down at it, and she laughed happily at his hesitation. 'You had to look, didn't you?'

'Yes,' he admitted, and she heard the smile. 'It's a blue background, with bright orange dragons.'

She laughed again, collected his arm, and moved forward. Wyatt watched the toes of his shoes move in steady, even strides in front of him, trying to block the sight of her smaller, patent leather sandals from his peripheral vision. The pressure of her hand on his arm seemed intolerably heavy and hot, although in reality it was only feather-light; and with each step they took, he imagined that their bodies drew closer and closer together. He stopped abruptly and removed his suit jacket, holding it out behind her—not so much because he thought she was cold, but because he was becoming unbearably warm. 'Here,' he commanded. 'Put this on.'

She complied willingly, and seemed to shrink under the added weight, wrapping it around her with a delighted shiver. 'Thank you. That's much better.'

But it wasn't better. Not for Wyatt. It was worse. Now only the thin fabric of his shirt lay between the skin of his arm and the warmth of her fingers, and he was more conscious than ever of her presence and her touch.

This is ridiculous, he thought angrily. Being this strongly attracted to a woman you've known only a few hours is patently ridiculous.

'There!' she said suddenly, stopping and cocking her head to listen. Her hair slipped over one shoulder with the gesture, and a long, curving strand of light flowed down over the rise of her breast. He couldn't pull his eyes away from looking at it. 'That's the noisemaker, isn't it?' she smiled. 'Windchimes! How lovely!'

She pulled him towards the sound and turned into the walk just opposite the delicate, musical tinkling. 'But what do you do when there's no wind?' she asked.

She's blind, he told himself. She's your patient, nothing else. She can never be anything else. 'Count from the fountain,' he answered in a normal voice. 'You can pace it off tomorrow. The fountain is exactly midway between the main house and the medical building.'

She nodded thoughtfully, and turned to face him. 'Do you go home now?'

'Yes.'

'And what happens tomorrow?'

'I'll meet you in the dining room for breakfast. At eight. Maggie will ring your room at seven.'

She sighed pensively and frowned. 'And tomorrow it begins, doesn't it?'

'In earnest.'

She shrugged lightly, looking very small in the heavy bulk of his jacket. 'Well. I know this sounds ridiculous, but I've had the most wonderful evening, in spite of ... everything,' she finished lamely.

He raised his eyebrows and smiled with the tolerance of an adult quietly amused at a child's pleasures. 'You're easily pleased,' he said gently.

'And sometimes, when you aren't trying not to be, you're easy to be with,' she responded, reaching up with her hands to find his face.

It was such a natural gesture, touching his face. She did it all the time, at home, to her father, the servants, Mrs Carmody. It meant hello, and goodbye, and a hundred other subtle things more eloquent than mere words could convey; things that blind people couldn't say with their eyes. And she had forgotten, for just a moment, that this was the man who had left her helpless by the creek; the man who had stung her with insults and mocked her insecurities. In the course of their walk he had become simply a companion; a person she could grow to like; and her gesture said that.

She felt his jaw tense under her hand, and her brows came together with the dismayed realisation that she had done something wrong. She let her hand fall from his face, then jumped at the sudden, brutal grasp of his fingers around hers, quivering with the effort of remaining motionless.

He was looking at her. She could feel his gaze through her blindness; feel the tension that crackled around them in that split second of his hesitation; then there was a rush of air against her face, and his lips touched hers, and then it was there again—that incredible, shuddering sensation that tore through her body like a New York subway, leaving her weak, and breathless, and absolutely incredulous.

She felt his lips soften from a fierce line and part, heard the sharp catch in his breath as her own lips followed his, and knew in that moment that as helpless as she was under his touch, he was equally so under hers. Here and now, at this moment, she was not blind, not an outcast, not different. With their eyes closed and their bodies touching, she was, for the very first time, simply a woman.

Wyatt felt her press against him, felt the hesitant response of her lips under his, then the air left his lungs in a convulsive shudder. He tore his mouth away and stood rigid, astounded at her power, bewildered by his helplessness. He squeezed his eyes shut and fought for control, and when he opened them, she was staring sightlessly forward, her face a portrait of hopeless confusion.

It wasn't supposed to happen. It had never happened before today, and it wasn't ever supposed to happen at all. And he had been prepared, he thought. Hardened with determination after his lapse of the afternoon, fully armed against her attraction as a woman, reminding himself constantly that she was a patient, and inviolate. But then her hand had touched his cheek, and her face had been poised just below his, tipped upward expectantly, touching him with eyes that couldn't see, driving him with forces beyond his control. And then their lips had touched, and it had been too late.

Remorse fought with anger as he struggled against emotions that made no sense whatsoever. It was all so natural for her, so easy. She simply responded, like a young, healthy animal, totally unaware of the professional relationship they must maintain; blissfully ignorant that he was failing in his responsibility as her psychiatrist. She was totally innocent, and he was totally guilty. Not only had he violated their relationship for the second time in one day; he had abused the trust of a young woman so naive that she was totally defenceless against the instincts of her own body.

'I'll need my coat,' he said harshly, hating himself, and letting the hate seep into his tone. He tried not to touch her as he helped her out of it.

'I'm sorry,' she stammered, dropping her chin, baffled by events and emotions that went far beyond her experience, understanding neither the kiss, nor the cold hostility that followed it.

'You have nothing to be sorry for,' he growled. 'It's not your fault that I can't control my reaction to you. It's mine.'

Cassie felt the air leave her body in a rush. What was he talking about, not being able to control his reaction to her? Was there something beyond the miserable, ugly deformity of her blindness? Something that could draw a man, make him respond, even . . . lose control? She rocked back on her heels, astounded by the possibility. It was the first time since the accident that she had felt a glimmer of self-worth, and it lit a fire inside that filled her with a miraculous glow.

'I'll see you at breakfast,' he was saying, and she blinked rapidly, trying to find her voice.

Well, look at you, Cassie, she thought in awe. No eyes, no money, no skills, no experience—but maybe you have something. She hadn't the faintest idea of what that something might be, and at that moment, she couldn't have cared less.

Suddenly the prospect of two weeks with this man wasn't so dreadful after all, and she rolled to the balls of her feet, poised on the brink of a great adventure.

'Breakfast,' she smiled, then moved towards the house, leaving Wyatt standing alone, his fists tightening into balls of frustration.

He glared at her back as she left him, watched her count her steps upward to the porch, and had the circumstances been different, he would have been pleased with the sudden confidence she exhibited in finding her own way to the door.

CHAPTER SIX

CASSIE leaned forward across the dressing table to run her fingers down the smooth surface of the mirror, wondering what she looked like, wondering if she would ever know.

Maggie's wake-up call at seven had come a full half-hour after she had got up, and now, at seven-thirty, she was dressed and ready to make her first trip downstairs by herself. 'Will you have coffee with me this morning, Maggie?' she had asked her on the phone. 'I can be down in thirty minutes, and we'll have some time together before Dr Field arrives.' But it might take another thirty minutes just to find the dining room, she thought ruefully. Then she shrugged off her apprehension. She had found her way to her room last night, after all. In another few days, the entire house would be just like home.

She closed her door softly behind her, and counted twenty steps down the hall to where the stairway would begin. She bumped her knuckles on the wall and shook her wrist against the sharp, tiny pain. She had overshot. She backed up two steps, and found the banister. Counting steps only worked if your steps were exactly the same size each time, and sighted people never realised how drastically mood could affect the length of your stride. This morning she was happy, and her stride had been too long.

She moved more carefully down the broad, curving staircase, and paused to savour the accomplishment when she reached the bottom. She remembered crossing a wide, open expanse of tile from yesterday, and trasversed it with short, mincing steps until she sensed a wall before her. Then she turned right, running her left hand along the waist-high wainscoting to guide her, and walked confidently to the first door. That was the music room, or so Maggie had identified it. She trailed her fingers across the space of the open doorway and walked on, smelling coffee and the Boston ferns at the same time. Just a few more steps and she could sense the subtle difference in the air around one of the voluminous plants, as the green fronds filled the narrow circle around them with a cool humidity detectable by only the most delicate instruments, and any blind person. She skirted the plant stand carefully, turned left to face the open space leading into the dining room, and lifted her chin expectantly.

Maggie hesitated in the motion of raising her coffee cup to her lips, and stared at the tiny figure framed in the wide doorway. Had Maggie O'Shea been less of a woman, or had Cassie Winters been more, Maggie would have felt the sickening tug of envy. As it was, Cassie's childlike innocence projected itself around the perfection of her face and her body, and evoked in Maggie a protective emotion that transcended envy. There was an alert anticipation about the blind girl, as if the world had just surprised her with something wonderful, and she could hardly wait to see what would happen next. Maggie smiled slightly as some of that anticipation crossed the room to infect her. She replaced her cup carefully in its saucer, and nodded silent approval as Cassie's head tipped immediately towards the muted sound. Then Cassie made her way slowly through the maze of tables scattered haphazardly throughout the room, wincing when she bumped her shin on an unforeseen obstacle, smiling when her hands found one first. Eventually she felt the back of the chair opposite Maggie's, and she exhaled strongly and grinned. 'Okay, Maggie. You can make a noise now. I know you're there.'

Maggie laughed and reached across the table to touch Cassie's hand. 'You did that very well,' she smiled. 'Almost gracefully. Where is yesterday's awkward, frightened blind woman?'

Cassie slipped quickly into her chair and leaned across the table. 'Oh, Maggie! I'm so glad I came!' she began breathlessly. 'The most wonderful things have been happening!'

Her excitement was contagious, and Maggie grinned as she shared it.

'I found my way back from the creek yesterday; I took a walk outside after dinner; I found you this morning without breaking even one leg, and . . .' She shrugged helplessly, her eyes bright, unable to articulate the joy of accomplishment, and unwilling to share the single revelation most responsible for her mood. One man had reacted to her as a woman—not as a blind woman, but just as a woman; and even warm, compassionate Maggie, with all her Irish empathy, would never be able to understand just what that had meant.

Maggie frowned and filled Cassie's coffee cup from a morning pot of sturdy crockery. They all went through this—the first, ebullient phase when they accomplished something on their own for the first time. There was no high to equal the blind's first taste of independence, and while they basked in the glow of that achievement, anything seemed possible. Poor Cassie. The glow would evaporate soon enough, when she learned she was just beginning, and that the worst lay ahead. Maggie's natural sympathetic nature rebelled at the prospect of seeing Cassie's joy shattered by reality, and she tried to temper the blow. 'You've accomplished a lot, Cassie; but now it's going to get harder. Wyatt will become even more demanding, and expect things of you that will seem impossible.'

Cassie shook her head with certainty. 'It doesn't matter, Maggie. I can do anything now. You don't understand.' Then she dismissed the subject with an impatient wave of her hand. 'But let's not talk about me. That's all I've known for years. My whole world has revolved around me, me, me. Tell me about you!'

Maggie's brows shot up in surprise. Rarely did

students express curiosity about the staff's personal lives. Their world seemed perpetually narrow, including only those things that affected them directly. Most of them thought of staff members as people who existed only in relation to their functions at the school, as if they had no life apart from it.

'What do you want to know?' she asked hesitantly, still expecting a question about her physical appearance, or how she came to work at Windrow.

'Well,' Cassie began, barely able to contain her curiosity, 'where do you live; what do you do when you aren't working here; do you have a boyfriend, or a husband; do you like animals...' she paused for a breath and laughed. 'Everything, Maggie! Tell me everything!'

Maggie joined in her laughter helplessly, and for the first time with any student she had tended, felt as if she were about to share confidences with a friend. And in that first moment of response, she paid Cassie one of the highest compliments she would ever unknowingly receive. She forgot she was blind.

'I live in a tiny house about a mile from here,' she began, 'although I only stay there on weekends. Otherwise I live here, as part of the job. It's kind of a gingerbread house, like the ones in picture books about Hansel and Gretel—did you ever see one of those?'

'Yes, yes! With fat roof shingles and windows with shutters—a cottage!'

'Exactly. It even has a picket fence, and window boxes, although the flowers are starting to fade now.'

'And what do you do there, on weekends?' Cassie was leaning forward eagerly, drinking in glimpses of another person's life, satisfying a thirst she had never been able to articulate; a thirst to know another human being outside the tiny circle of her isolation.

Maggie relayed a detailed, comical description of spending half of every Saturday dusting away cobwebs that had accumulated in her week-long absence, and she and Cassie were both giggling when Wyatt appeared in the doorway.

Maggie caught his eye almost immediately, and her smile faded into an expression of wary confusion. He was dressed meticulously in pressed jeans and a black turtleneck sweater, but he was unshaven, and a dark shadow covered the lower half of his face. It was as if he had paid careful, exhausting attention to his appearance as he dressed, but had been distracted, and simply forgot to shave. The effect would have been the same if a woman appeared at a formal dinner in gown and jewels, completely made-up, with her hair still in rollers. And it was not like Wyatt to be careless. Not like him at all.

His eyes were narrowed against the light in the dining room, and he stood unnaturally stiff in the doorway, his expression stern, his entire posture forbidding.

Cassie was frowning, wondering why Maggie had stopped speaking in mid-sentence.

'Good morning, Wyatt,' Maggie said quietly, questioning him with her eyes.

Cassie brightened at the mention of his name, and turned around in her chair as if she could see him. 'Good morning!' she called out gaily, and Wyatt's face seemed to darken even more.

He approached the table with a reluctance that bordered on distaste, and stood next to Maggie with long lines of tension pulling down at his mouth. 'Did you dress her this morning, too, or did she manage that on her own?' he demanded harshly, ignoring Cassie's presence as if she were deaf as well as blind. Before either woman could protest, he snapped, 'I told you she was not to be led around, and it's obvious you brought her in here, or she would have left a trail of overturned chairs.'

Maggie gasped at the undeserved reprimand, so astounded to be chastised in front of a patient that she could not respond. She glanced at Cassie, her anger rising to fury when she saw her wounded, confused expression. She rose so quickly that her chair rocked before settling to the stability of its four legs, her face flaming with a colour close to that of her hair. 'Cassie,' she said steadily, while looking directly at Wyatt. 'I know well enough when to bite my tongue on my temper. If I said anything now, I'd regret it later, so I'll leave the explanations to you. I couldn't trust myself to make them.' And with that she stomped off briskly, her tight, red curls bouncing.

Wyatt stared after her, his jaw clenched; then slid into the chair she had vacated. He poured himself a cup of coffee, then glanced up at Cassie.

She wore a light, shimmering sweater that reflected the colour of her eyes, and he felt his resentment intensify, feeling that every garment she owned was worn with the intent to arouse him. 'Good morning, Ms Winters,' he said coldly, and averted his gaze.

'You owe Maggie an apology,' she said timidly, and his eyes jerked up to glare at her.

'My working relationship with Maggie is none of your concern,' he said icily.

'But you're wrong about this morning. I dressed myself, and I found my way to this table myself. Maggie waited exactly where you're sitting. She never helped me.'

'I'll see that you both get gold stars,' he said drily, and Cassie cringed at the unexpected contempt in his voice. 'Now let's order breakfast, and get on with your treatment. You're not here to socialise, Ms Winters, as I've told you before. You're here to learn.'

His open hostility confounded her completely, and Cassie's face mirrored exactly how she felt—like a bewildered puppy suffering punishment for some unknown error.

She had spent a long, sleepless hour in bed last night, analysing the perplexing behaviour of this man, and had reached her own, happy conclusion. That encounter by the creek had *not* been part of her treatment; nor had the episode last night. For some impossible, unknown reason, Dr Field was attracted to her; and from now on her therapy was to have been a two-week blossoming of a relationship destined to be special—perhaps ultimate—and there would be no more tension between them.

But he wasn't following the script. There was more in his manner than a residual anger at himself for losing control; much more. Inexplicably, he hated her. She could feel the waves of hatred pounding against the thin wall of self-esteem she had built only the night before, and like the fragile structure it was, it crumbled almost immediately.

Stupid, stupid blind girl! she chided herself silently. Thinking you could ever appeal to such a man!

Wyatt watched in grim satisfaction as Cassie's expression shifted from confusion to a blank stare of resignation. This morning was easy. Being cruel was easy. He watched her face carefully as it reflected all the emotions assaulting her mind, and savoured her suffering, because he did hate her. In that moment, he hated her as strongly as he had ever hated anything. He resented the power she had to make him lose control, almost totally, twice in one day. He hated the power of her presence to trouble his sleep, to intrude into his thoughts, to make him question his own worth as a psychiatrist.

Had he been a weaker man, he would have acknowledged his senseless emotional attraction to this girl, and removed himself from her case. But that would have been an admission of defeat, and Wyatt Field did not accept defeat easily. It would be agonising to spend almost every hour of every day in her company, while maintaining professional distance, and so that was the course he chose. Whatever it required, he would crush the awesome power of his own emotions; and whatever it required, he would unlock the secrets of that closed mind of hers, and force Cassie Winters to see again.

They ate breakfast in silence, she pushing food around her plate in gestures that were only an imitation of eating; he eagerly devouring each morsel, as if satisfying one physical need would quiet another.

'What do you remember about your mother?' he asked abruptly after their plates were removed by a formless presence Cassie could not identify.

'Where's Helen?' she asked, ignoring his question

'She starts at eleven, and the hours the staff keeps are not your concern. I asked you a question.'

She caught her lower lip between her teeth and frowned. 'Why are you so angry with me?' she asked hesitantly. 'What have I done wrong?'

His laugh was cold. 'What have *you* done? Do you think my entire life revolves around Cassie Winters? Can the only reason for my behaviour be something involving you? It's time you learned, Ms Winters, that you're not the centre of anyone's existence but your own. Remember that.'

The denial had been too vehement. Anyone more experienced would have recognised that, but to Cassie, his words were a resounding slap in the face. She looked down quickly and fussed with the napkin in her lap. When she could trust herself to speak, she asked, 'Are all blind people so self-centred, or is it only me?'

He closed his eyes against the despair in her voice, and the dejection of her bent head, and chastised himself silently. He was being too hard on her. He knew that, but was powerless to control it. If he relented, even a little, he would be incapable of treating her at all. 'Tell me about your mother,' he repeated, refusing to even acknowledge her question.

Cassie's shoulders slumped with the force of her sigh. 'She was beautiful,' she whispered. 'Not like a fashion model, or a movie star—not that kind of beauty. Something softer. Like a painting of the Madonna that you see in church.' She lifted her face, caught up in the visual memory behind eyes that seemed to bore through Wyatt, focusing on some point in the distant past. 'Everything about her was soft, and quiet. Her eyes, her smile, her voice . . . you know, I can't remember ever hearing her raise her voice. Not once. That's extraordinary, isn't it?' A slight smile touched her lips, and Wyatt knew she was no longer speaking to him, but only musing aloud. 'I remember once when I caught a small snake in the field behind our house, and I brought it to my mother where she was sitting in the lawn chair. I knew she was afraid of snakes, so I didn't come too close; I just held it out for her to see. She looked at the snake, then she looked at me and smiled, and told me it was very pretty, but probably frightened, and that I should put it down gently so it could go home to its family.' Cassie paused and chuckled, shaking her head.

'So I put it down carefully, and we both watched the snake slither away, and then she jumped up and ran to me, and carried me all the way up to the house. We studied snake books for the next two weeks, until she was sure I would never pick up a copperhead again.'

'Good God!'

Cassie's smile widened at his involuntary exclamation. 'She was remarkable that way. She always did exactly the right thing. Always.'

Wyatt was silent for a moment, imagining the quiet strength of the woman Cassie was describing, wondering at what cost she found the courage to keep from screaming when she saw the lethal snake in her daughter's hands. 'What kind of a relationship did you and your mother have?' he asked finally.

'It was ... close. Very close. I never wanted to be anywhere but where she was. And Father, of course. We were all close. But with Mother, it was something more, something special. Not just because she was my mother, but because she was ... my favourite person. Can you understand that?' Cassie leaned forward in her earnestness, suddenly desperate to convey to someone else the qualities she remembered in a woman dead for nearly two decades. 'She was always there; always ready to hear anything I had to say, as if it were the most important, most interesting thing in the world. She always listened.'

Her sigh was ragged, and escaped her lips in short little jerks that made her nostrils flare. 'Could we talk about something else?' she asked weakly, her eyes a bright, moist plea that pierced Wyatt like a blade.

'Where were you going the night of the accident?' he asked gruffly.

Cassie blanched, and swallowed the lump in her throat. 'I . . . I don't know. I can't remember.'

'That day, then. What did you do that day?'

Her forehead wrinkled, straining against the recollection of a time long since buried, her eyes wide to contain tears threatening to spill over, her lips pressed into a hard line of white. 'I practised the piano,' she said tremulously, surprising herself at the memory, wondering where it had come from. 'Mother and I always practised the piano together in the mornings. She was teaching me.' Her voice faded to a low whisper.

'What song?' he demanded. 'What song were you learning? What song did you play that morning?'

Her lips quivered and her fingers tightened around the napkin in her lap. Her knuckles whitened as nearly transparent skin stretched taut over the bones. The melody reverberated in her mind, coming from nowhere, threading faintly through a piercing ringing sound that was becoming louder and louder, until the melody throbbed in booming, deafening chords to be heard over the ringing. Both sounds battled in her ears until her hands flew up to press tight against them, to stop the screeching discord, to push the noise back into her head. Her eyes squeezed shut against the pain of sounds so loud they threatened to burst her eardrums, and she had to be scream to be heard over it. 'Beethoven! The Moonlight Sonata!' she cried, and the sound inside her head stopped.

She dropped her hands from her ears, and her eyes flew open in amazement. The dining room was deathly still, holding its breath, and the silence was somehow frightening. 'I didn't know that,' she whispered, staring. 'I didn't know that. I never play Beethoven.'

Wyatt smoothed the tension lines in his forehead with a hand that trembled, feeling the explosion of her release as surely as if it had been his own. 'Let's take a walk, Cassie,' he said quietly, and neither of them noticed that he had used her first name.

Cassie literally jumped to her feet, suddenly filled with a frantic, nervous energy she could not contain. Her face was pale, her eyes still wide and frightened, and she turned to rush impulsively from the room, forgetting that blind people never rush anywhere. The urge to escape was so strong that it crowded out any logical process of thought, and she ran headlong into a fully set table, pushed herself aside, then immediately tripped over a chair. She was not reasoning now, only running. Running from whatever called back memories too painful to endure; running from the man who would force her to remember what her mind had decided should be forgotten. She was dimly aware of the painful crack of her pelvis against something wooden and unyielding, and tried desperately to push through the barrier, to make herself a part of the wood, until Wyatt's voice stopped her, slicing through the air like the crack of a whip.

'Cassie! Stop!'

She felt his hands on her arms; pushing, steering, guiding her through the tables and chairs, across the spacious foyer, out to the porch and down the steps. She breathed deeply of the morning air in irregular gasps, rubbing her hands together against a chill that had no place in the warm sunshine.

Wyatt stood quietly by, watching her regain her composure, struggling against the impulse to take her into his arms.

'Well,' she said shakily. 'That isn't a scene I'll look back on with pride.'

'You should,' he answered gently. 'And you will. We have to talk about it.'

'I'd rather not.' Her voice quivered with apprehension.

'I'm afraid that doesn't make a bit of difference. You're going to.'

A tiny muscle tightened in her cheek, and he smiled slowly at her silent gesture of defiance. 'You faced a small piece of the memory your mind has suppressed, and you dealt with it. That's something to be proud of. And it's a beginning. You can't stop now.'

'Maybe being blind is better,' she said flatly. 'If a piano piece was that devastating to remember, the rest must be unbearable.'

'It was—to a child's mind. But you're a mature woman now, capable of accepting things that would have destroyed you then. Besides, it may not be as horrible as you imagine.'

'Can you guarantee that?' she asked desperately, demanding an unreasonable promise to quiet her growing fear.

He closed his eyes briefly, and when he answered, his voice was steady. 'No. Of course I can't. But it's the only chance you have. Now then.' The lightness in his tone sounded only slightly strained. 'If we go back to the creek, do you promise to keep your shoes on?'

She brightened almost immediately, and Wyatt watched her features lift, eradicating all trace of former worry as if it had never existed. She had the resilience of a child, it seemed; as well as the naiveté of one, and that was good.

'On second thought,' he continued, appraising her rapid recovery from that first, staggering piece of memory, and deciding to move faster, 'we'll go somewhere else. The highway, perhaps.'

'The highway?' she asked uncertainly, instinctively wary of anything new. 'Why not back to the creek? At least it was pleasant there, and I know how to get to it.'

'Exactly why we aren't going there,' he said firmly. 'Now take us to the highway.'

She narrowed her eyes slightly, considering, then shrugged and reached out to slip her hand through his arm.

'No!' he shouted, jerking his arm away violently, and she jumped backwards a step. 'On your own!' he commanded. She should have responded with hostile fury to his sudden harshness, but instead, she just stood there, looking wounded.

Fight, dammit! he commanded her silently. Don't just stand there! Fight back!

He forced sarcastic cruelty into his voice while his eyes watched her with hopeful expectation. 'What's wrong, Ms Winters? Can't you manage anything on your own? Perhaps you were right after all. Perhaps you should leave Windrow, and return to that Park Avenue cocoon of yours. I could use some time off anyway. Babysitting bores me.'

Cassie's troubled features relaxed into a mask that revealed nothing. 'All right, Dr Field,' she said quietly. 'The highway it is. Maybe I'll get lucky and you'll step in front of a speeding truck.'

Some of the darkness in Wyatt's face lifted as his mouth turned up in a sardonic smile.

Cassie sidled across the walk until the slight ridge of the kerb bumped her foot. She stepped down carefully on to the road's surface, and began to walk with short, mincing steps, guided by the side of her right foot as she nudged up to the kerb. Wyatt followed a few paces behind, wondering how long it would take before the fear of walking into nothingness would stop her. It took longer than he expected. They were nearly halfway to that point where Windrow's private drive turned out on to the main highway before Cassie stopped suddenly.

'I'm not going any further,' she said firmly. 'This is impossible.'

'You're almost there. Keep walking.'

She took one more step, then stopped again. 'No. You don't know what you're asking.' Her voice quivered only slightly.

'I'm not asking. I'm telling. Now keep walking.'

'No!' she shouted, spinning around. 'What for?'

'Because you're afraid.'

'Of course I'm afraid!' she shrilled. 'I'm walking into a black hole! An endless void! That would terrify anyone! Why can't you understand that?'

'I understand all too well, Ms Winters,' he said quietly, the control of his voice underscoring the hysterical quality of hers. 'You're afraid to face the future; afraid to face the past; afraid of a simple walk down a country road. You're afraid of everything. What it all boils down to, is that you're afraid of life. What I don't understand is why you haven't killed yourself long before now.'

Cassie's eyes widened incredulously at the absolute indifference in his voice, and for the first time in her life she believed in the existence of people who could remain totally untouched by human suffering. 'You're incredible!' she whispered involuntarily, feeling the sickness of one who has just encountered a nightmare, and learned that it had a name, and a face, and a body. 'You have no compassion at all; no feeling at all. Nothing touches you. You're the one who should commit suicide, not I,' she continued, shaking her head in disbelief. 'What on earth do you have to live for?'

Wyatt smiled grimly, and let her accusations wash over him without penetrating. He could feel the beginning of her hatred like a tangible presence, and it pleased him.

Cassies raised the fingers of one hand to her lips, suddenly thinking of something that had not occurred to her before. 'You hate us, don't you?' she whispered. 'All blind people. And the hatred is a sickness even you can't control. It's made you hard.'

Wyatt flinched only slightly. 'It's an occupational hazard of dealing with people like you,' he answered evenly. 'Useless people, who have nothing to offer but constant need; no excuse for living at all.' He paused briefly to check her reaction, and when he saw her stiffen, determined to endure his insults with stoic indifference, he intensified the disdain in his voice. 'You burden your families and your friends with your helplessness, and wallow in the sympathy you receive from strangers. You exist in constant fear, deserting the people who need you, turning inward until you aren't even aware of a world outside yourselves; and when it becomes too difficult, you simply drop out. Stop living. Either figuratively, or literally. Actually, it would be a kindness if you all killed yourselves right away, instead of putting the people around you through the slow torture of lingering death. Because that's what you are when you refuse to fight, refuse to try to live—you're dead already. You only pretend to be alive.'

Cassie's mouth hung open in disbelief as she tried to absorb the impact of all he had said. It's just a psychiatric ploy, she kept telling herself. He's trying to make you mad, fighting mad. It's the oldest trick in the book. Part of her believed that; but another part, that part fed by senses developed and honed to a fine perception by her blindness, told her that subconsciously, he meant every word. His hatred for blind people, or at least those blind who refused to help themselves, was frighteningly real.

She whispered her question, almost afraid to hear the answer, and her words were thick with a sympathy that Wyatt found totally offensive. 'Who was the blind person who hurt you so much?'

Wyatt's head jerked back on his shoulders in surprise. She was entirely too perceptive, and the accuracy of her intuition hit him like an unexpected hammer blow. No one, not even the staff, had ever suspected the blind woman in his past, and now a girl he had known for only a matter of hours had cleanly cut through all the pretence and sensed the ugliness behind him—just like that. He felt naked and defenceless, as if she could read his mind, and the sensation was repugnant. There was no privacy in a relationship where one party could always sense the motivations of the other. No privacy at all. It was one reason he had never allowed himself to become close to anyone. He gave no indication of his seething emotions when he spoke.

'Do you blame your father for your mother's death?' he asked calmly, and Cassie reeled under the unexpected question, forgetting everything else that had been said, just as he had planned she would.

'No,' she whispered, repressing the same impulse to flee that had sent her careening through the dining room earlier.

'Do you blame yourself?'

'No!'

'Do you remember being in the car? Sitting with your mother? Did she scream? Did you?'

His questions came rapid-fire, hitting her mind like sharp, unrelenting fists, and she backed away from him slowly, her eyes wide, her mouth open, whispering over and over, 'No! No! No!'

Suddenly the questions stopped, and Cassie stood trembling in anticipation, waiting for the onslaught to continue. There was silence for a time, and other sounds began to crack the shield of her consciousness. Birds, in a nearby tree; the skittering noise a dry leaf made as it danced across the tar in front of her; the steady drone of grasshoppers heralding the end of summer. Her breathing slowed as she waited for him to speak, knowing his eyes were on her.

'Let's go back,' he said finally, but when he turned to retrace their steps, she remained standing, holding her secrets inside, considering his words in a larger scope than he had intended. She could not go back. She could never go back. There was nothing there.

'I'm going to the highway,' she said quietly, and turned and began the slow, pathetic, kerb-bumping gait with a silent determination that made the action seem almost gallant.

Wyatt followed her in silence, his face revealing nothing.

CHAPTER SEVEN

CASSIE hunched over the writing desk in her room, laboriously feeling the raised lines on her braille tablet with the fingers of her left hand as she printed with her right. The letters were uneven, and childish, and sometimes words ran together and on top of one another as she misjudged spaces, but for the most part, the letter was remarkably legible.

'Dear Mrs Carmody,

I have been promised a typewriter, so my next letter will be longer, and easier to read, but I couldn't wait to tell you how much I miss you. Windrow is beautiful—at least it feels beautiful—and the doctors here tell me there is still a chance I might see again. If that happens, our problems will not be so insurmountable. Please don't make any definite plans yet. We have three months after I am released from here before the lease runs out. That will give us enough time to plan. The money will last that long. Give my love to Robert.'

She leaned back heavily against the chair, and thought about what she had written. She was kidding herself, of course. Even if she regained her sight, how could she possibly afford to retain Mrs Carmody? What kind of a job could she find that would bring in enough income to justify a housekeeper?

She smiled cryptically at the thought of Mrs Carmody being labelled as a housekeeper. It was an almost unforgivable understatement. It was what she had been, of course, back when she was hired when Cassie was a baby. Stiff, proper, unbending Mrs Carmody. But after the accident, she became much more. The rock around which she and her father revolved; a prim, reserved woman trying vainly to be the mother Cassie had lost; the eyes she no longer had; the friends she would never make. Housekeeper, indeed!

And then came that extraordinary, unbelievable day when the lawyers delivered the final blow after the death of her father, and Cassie's world shattered around her. Mrs Carmody had been there, as always, to pick up the pieces.

'I tried, Ms Winters,' the portly lawyer had said apologetically. 'But it was hopeless. There was no talking to your father; not after the accident.' There were long pauses between his sentences, and Cassie sensed a sincere regret in the man's kindly manner. 'The wealth he enjoyed as a young man was considerable, it's true,' he had continued, 'and with careful attention it would have increased through the years. In spite of the fact that he stopped practising law after the accident, there would have been enough, managed properly, to keep all of you comfortable for the rest of your lives.' He hesitated again, and cleared his throat. 'But he refused to make concessions; refused to alter his lifestyle; and in essence, his continued extravagance was financial suicide. It couldn't have gone on much longer, even if he had lived. He had already borrowed on most of his life insurance policies. Only the small one remaining saved the estate from bankruptcy.'

'So there's nothing left,' Mrs Carmody had said perfunctorily.

'I'm afraid that's correct.'

'Nothing at all for Cassie.'

'Just a small trust fund established years ago by her mother. It was the one thing he couldn't touch. It, at least, remained intact, and gathered interest. It isn't much, but at least it's something.'

He had named a figure, but Cassie was beyond hearing by that time. She knew nothing of finances. She had never had to know. Money had always been there, and it had never occurred to her that one day it might not be.

'Well,' Mrs Carmody had sniffed, 'so much for the loving father. And to think I used to pity the man!'

'He deserved your pity,' the lawyer had interjected quietly. 'Believe me, Mrs Carmody; he did. He was just never the same after the accident. I don't think he ever fully realised what he was doing.'

'But that doesn't help Cassie much, now does it?' Mrs Carmody had countered angrily. Then she had turned to Cassie, and there must have been something in the stricken face that touched her, that made her realise that was not the time to rant against a dead man; because she brushed her hands together in that brisk, no-nonsense manner of hers, and tried to mend the situation with sheer bravado.

'It won't be so bad, Cassie. There's enough to pay for your treatment at that school, for one thing . . . what was the name? . . . ah, yes. Windrow. And maybe they can put it all right. And there will be a bit left over. We'll let the staff go immediately, of course, that will give us a little extra; and then I'll find another position, only I won't live in. You and I will find a nice, cosy apartment somewhere, and we'll do just fine. You'll see.'

Cassie had managed a weak smile, covering her desperate effort to understand. She tried to forgive her father's incredible irresponsibility; but the first, un-reasoning flash of hatred; the first clear image of a despicably weak man, pretending to be strong at the expense of those who trusted him, settled in her mind, and she had been fighting it ever since.

He did love me; he *did*, she had tried to convince herself a dozen times in the last week. He was just weak, and lost, and you can't blame a man for that, can you?

Of the two of them, he had been more handicapped. She realised that now. Using her as an excuse to crawl into a protective shell where he could live out his years without a single reminder of the past, simply waiting to

die. He had been dying, after all, since the accident;
without foresight, without thinking what his refusal to
go on with the business of living would do to Cassie.

She recalled telling Dr Field that she loved her father,
and realisation came with a shudder that the father she
loved had been dead for eighteen years, not just two
weeks. Wyatt's words crept unbidden into her mind . . .
'You exist in constant fear, deserting the people who
need you, turning inward until you aren't even aware of
a world outside yourselves . . .' She smiled bitterly. He
had been describing the blind, but what he had really
described was her father, not her. Her only fault had
been to depend on him; to trust in an empty shell that
had nothing left to give.

Cassie rose from the desk, and with one violent sweep
of her hand, knocked everything to the floor. There was
no future in depending on anyone. She would never
make that mistake again.

She felt the raised symbols on her wristwatch, and
began the methodical preparations to go downstairs for
lunch. Dr Field had given her an hour alone after that
dreadful walk to the highway, and the time was almost
up.

'Good Lord, Wyatt! If I didn't know better, I'd say
you were hung over.' Dr Franklin peered over the
tops of his glasses, frowning with disapproval as the
younger man entered his office and sank into the
chair opposite his desk. 'Has anyone bothered to tell
you you forgot to shave this morning, or was it an
intentional oversight?'

Wyatt's hand darted up to his cheek, and rubbed
back and forth across the black stubble. 'I didn't
notice,' he mumbled. 'I was in a hurry this morning.'

Dr Franklin chuckled and leaned back in his chair,
removing his glasses and rubbing his eyes with the
thumb and forefinger of one hand. 'Does the enigmatic
Dr Field actually have a secret night life? If so, I hope it
was half as good as you look bad this morning.'

'I worked last night.' The reply was almost a snap, and Franklin raised his brows in surprise.

'Sorry,' Wyatt said quickly. 'I'm having some ... unusual problems.'

Franklin knew better than to ask outright what the problems were, and sat quietly, worrying over the tiny tension lines around Wyatt's eyes. 'Anything you want to talk about?' he asked finally, deeming that a harmless question.

'No. I just stopped by to see if you'd had any luck finding a case similar to the Winters girl.'

Matt tightened his lips in exasperation. 'Nothing yet, but I've got calls out all over the country. If there's ever been a case like it, I'll find it. You're as much in the dark as your patient for a change, aren't you, Wyatt?'

Wyatt jumped from his chair in an explosion of nervous energy, and began to pace back and forth in front of the desk. 'I'm not sure how to treat her, Matt,' he complained bitterly. 'Not without guidelines. Everything I do is just guesswork without someone else's experience to go by. What if I push too hard, and she snaps, locking whatever it is inside forever? Or what if I don't push hard enough, and we accomplish nothing? She'll never try it again.'

Matt watched the angry pacing with concern, disturbed by the unusual intensity of Wyatt's reaction. 'Your instincts are usually reliable,' he said carefully, 'and normally you trust them. Why do you doubt them now?'

Wyatt came to an abrupt halt in front of the desk, closing his eyes, controlling his physical need to release tension with a massive effort. He blew a long breath out through his lips, and the squared shoulders relaxed slightly. 'You're right,' he said steadily. 'I'm over-reacting. It's just that there's a lot more to digging up horrors from someone's mind than there is to teaching blind people confidence. I haven't seen this side of psychiatry for a while, and I'm not used to it.'

Matt flashed a reassuring smile, wanting desperately to reach out and comfort his troubled young friend.

'It's perfectly understandable, Wyatt. It's an emotional strain, as much for the psychiatrist as it is for the patient—this reaching into the unknown, exposing all the ugly things the mind wants to keep locked away. You have to hurt them to help them, and guilt is a natural byproduct.' He lowered his eyes, then looked up at Wyatt cautiously. 'It's especially hard to hurt this one, isn't it?' he asked softly.

Wyatt's eyes narrowed dangerously, then he took a deep breath and allowed his features to relax. 'You're playing the psychiatrist's psychiatrist, Matt,' he said with a wry smile.

Dr Franklin shrugged and grinned sheepishly. 'Sorry. Are you making any progress with her?'

'Maybe too much. She remembered something this morning—just a little thing—a song she was playing on the piano the day of the accident; but the result was almost disastrous.'

'It's a beginning, then.'

Wyatt's voice was uncertain. 'Or the end. I caught her off-guard this time. Somehow I don't think that will happen again, and if her mind throws up its defences against me, I don't have a chance.'

'Are you sure you're not pushing her too fast?'

'No,' he answered grimly. 'I'm not sure.' He walked to the door and hesitated, his hand on the knob. 'I'd like to bring her to dinner Friday night, Matt. Would you mind? I'd like to see her in a family situation: see how she reacts to a mother figure. Katy's the best mother I know.'

'No problem. Katy will be delighted. I hope it helps.'

'So do I. Thanks.'

Matt sat quietly at his desk for a long time after the door had closed, tapping the end of his pen against a stack of unfinished reports. You must be getting old, Matthew Franklin, he chided himself. An old derelict given to wild flights of fancy and an overactive imagination. But what would prompt such preposterous notions, he wondered, unless there really *had* been something just a little odd in Wyatt's tone; a little out of the ordinary in the way his voice caught when he said her name; in the way his eyes shifted downward as though they would reveal too much? And even as an intense young man, had he ever been quite that intense before? That desperate to succeed, as if his own life depended on it?

He pondered for a moment, then made his decision, and picked up the phone to call Katy. He would only tell her what Wyatt had said—that he was bringing a patient along Friday to observe in a home environment. Katy would be able to either confirm or alleviate his suspicions without any prompting or advance knowledge, and he would be satisfied with that. Her judgment in such things was infallible.

Cassie was instantly aware of Wyatt's presence in the dining room, even though the minor sounds of his entrance had been totally obscured by the noises of the other diners. She lifted her eyes unerringly in his direction, her lips parted expectantly. It was a startling revelation, the ability to sense his presence; and although she wondered at the phenomenon, she didn't question it. He had not spoken, no one had called his name; but she knew he was there, as if every sense had been specifically attuned to seeking out this one man.

Wyatt's eyes found her a full thirty feet away, facing him from the room's farthest table. He knew from her expression that his nearly soundless entrance had not gone unnoticed. There were over a dozen people in the room, and of all of them, only one knew he was there, and that person was blind.

She looked very small from this distance, and very vulnerable. He noticed that she had changed from the sweater she had worn earlier to a lightweight blouse, and berated himself silently for noticing at all.

'I knew you were here,' she said simply as he took the chair opposite her. The blouse draped in a wide scoop over her shoulders, like the peasant blouses common to the Southwest, accentuating the slender column of her neck, drawing his eyes to the tiny pulse that beat in the hollow of her throat.

'Why shouldn't you?' he asked brusquely. 'I didn't make any effort to conceal my presence.'

He almost balked at the lie. Why was he lying to her anyway? He wouldn't have done that with any other patient.

'I don't understand it,' she persisted. 'Before you entered the room, I knew you were there, standing in the doorway, watching me.'

He remained perfectly still, saying nothing for a moment, feeling as unprofessional as he had ever felt in his career. 'Sixth sense,' he said finally, dismissing the importance of her observation. 'It's not so extraordinary with the blind. And you're not blind, after all. Not your eyes, anyway. Only your mind.'

She nodded slowly, digesting what he had said.

She had changed her hair, too. It was pulled away from her face, caught back in a long ponytail that rested on the nape of her neck, bringing her features into sharp relief. It made her eyes seem even larger, shaded by a thick fringe of naturally dark lashes that cast long, delicate shadows over her cheeks when she blinked.

'You're staring at me,' she said suddenly.

'So what?' he countered sharply, disturbed by her uncanny perception of what he was doing at any given moment.

The harshness of his tone baffled her, and her face reflected confusion, then indignation. 'So it's rude,' she snapped.

His low chuckle sent a shiver down the back of her neck. 'Surely you're used to being stared at.'

'Of course I'm used to it!' she hissed bitterly. 'Blind people are always stared at! That doesn't make it less rude, and you of all people, should know better!'

'I'm not staring because you're blind Ms Winters,' he said evenly. 'I'm staring because you're beautiful.'

She stilled immediately, and only the slight upward motion of the inside corners of her eyebrows gave any indication of her uncertainty.

'I see the compliment makes you uncomfortable,' Field said quietly. 'It shouldn't. It's time you knew what you looked like. Do you remember the colour of your hair? Your eyes?'

Cassie nodded slowly, her mind racing ahead, trying to see where the conversation was leading.

'Your eyes are quite startling, really,' he continued. 'I don't think I've ever seen a colour like it. And they're an extraordinary contrast to that hair of yours, which has almost no colour at all. It's as if an artist drew the outlines of your face, but coloured only the eyes, and left the rest blank. And you're too pale, of course. Almost pallid. Didn't you ever get outside?'

As if to defy his words, Cassie's cheeks filled with colour. 'I think I've had enough of the description, thank you. I'd rather not know what I look like, than hear it from you.'

Wyatt frowned. 'Flattery disturbs you?'

'Flattery! That was flattery? That I'm colourless?'

He was silent for a long moment, and when he finally spoke, his voice was professionally detached. 'Most of my patients are very uncertain about their appearance. The blind tend to believe that blindness itself is a disfigurement, and until they believe that their physical appearance is not repulsive, they lack the confidence to accomplish anything positive.'

'So you tell all of us that we're beautiful,' she said contemptuously.

'Not at all. My last patient lost her sight when her face went through the windshield in an automobile accident. What was left was hardly beautiful, but it wasn't nearly as horrible as her imagination had convinced her it was. Once she realised that, she was fine. I never told her she was beautiful. It would have been a cruel lie. I told you you were beautiful because you are. It was simply the truth.'

Cassie fidgeted in her chair, uncomfortable at the words which should have been complimentary, but weren't, because the delivery had been so indifferent. She raised her head suddenly, remembering something. 'Is that why you kissed me?' she asked innocently. 'Because I'm beautiful?'

The question was guileless, and unexpected, and caught him totally off-guard. He cleared his throat noisily and shifted in his chair. 'I suppose so,' he mumbled, then bit his lip angrily that his reply had sounded so lame.

'Do you kiss all of your patients?'

'Of course not!'

'Just the beautiful ones?'

Her questions were delivered with the artless curiosity of one who seeks simply to understand an unfamiliar custom. For some reason, that made responding to them all the more difficult.

He pressed his lips tightly together while his mind formulated a careful, harmless explanation; one that would not jeopardise their relationship as doctor and patient. 'It should never have happened,' he said finally, 'but since it did, there's no point in pretending. You're a beautiful young woman, and I would be lying if I asked you to believe that I didn't respond to that—on a very basic level. But that level has no place in our relationship as doctor and patient. Do you understand?'

'No.'

He closed his eyes and exhaled sharply in exasperation. 'Just think of it as a mistake, Ms Winters. That's all. A mistake that won't happen again.'

She dropped her eyes slowly, and nodded once. On the table, Wyatt's hand tightened into a fist of white tension.

He sighed with relief when Helen approached the table, grateful for a diversion of any sort. 'I'll have whatever Ms Winters ordered, Helen.'

Helen's voice was cold, and unmistakably annoyed.

'She hasn't ordered yet, Dr Field. We've been keeping the kitchen open for some time now.'

'I'm sorry, Helen,' Cassie put in quickly. 'I didn't realise . . . I was just waiting for Dr Field.'

Wyatt scowled at Helen, baffled by her unusual behaviour. 'There's no need to appologise, Cassie,' he said slowly, looking pointedly at Helen. 'The staff is here for your convenience; not the other way around. Isn't that right, Helen?'

'Of course,' she responded icily, a flush diffusing the rich olive complexion.

'It doesn't matter,' Cassie said hastily, confused by the hostile vibrations battering the air around her. 'I'll have the lamb, Helen. Thank you.'

Wyatt held up two fingers and frowned as Helen nodded curtly, then stalked away.

Sometimes Cassie's senses were remarkably acute, and sometimes they failed her completely. Now, for instance, although she could hear Wyatt's steady breathing less than a foot away, although she could feel the subtle changes in the air currents when he moved, she had no idea what he was looking at. It reminded her of listening to televison programmes, knowing that without sight, she was missing something important. 'Would it be a violation of your rules if you told me something about yourself?' she asked softly.

She sensed his eyes moving to touch her, and imagined his suspicious frown.

'Just what is it you'd like to know?'

Cassie pressed her lips into a tight line, considering what she would ask. 'When you have time,' she said finally, 'time for yourself; time away from your work; what do you like to do more than anything else?'

There was silence for a moment, then she heard him fuss with his napkin. 'I've never had that kind of time,' he answered brusquely.

'Every waking minute is devoted to your work?'

'Every one.'

She pondered that for a moment, then wrinkled her

nose in distaste. 'Sounds dull,' she pronounced, and he laughed.

'I'm often accused of being just that.'

'Is that why you've never married?'

'Maybe.'

'Have you ever been in love?'

Wyatt looked up sharply and examined her face for a trace of facetiousness, but found it seriously attentive. 'Once,' he said earnestly. 'With my fourth grade teacher. I never got over it.'

She gave him a small smile on cue and shrugged. 'All right. Be mysterious.'

'I'm not trying to be mysterious. My personal life just has nothing to do with our relationship, that's all. There's no point to discussing it.'

Coincidentally, her eyes moved without hesitation until she seemed to be staring directly into his. 'You know,' she said, 'it's a funny thing about being blind. You develop this animal-like sense of how people react to you. It's hard to explain, and I can't tell you where the signals come from, but they're there, just as surely as if you could see them. Maggie, for instance. Maggie liked me immediately, and I think we'll be good friends. And Dr Franklin, even though we spent only a short time together, feels an almost fatherly protectiveness toward me.' She was interrupted as Helen served their meal in sullen silence, and waited for her to move out of earshot before continuing. 'And Helen,' she went on, 'Helen resents me; almost hates me. But you, Dr Field,' she paused as she lifted her fork, 'you're afraid of me. No one has ever been afraid of me before.'

Wyatt sat absolutely still, composing in his mind first an angry denial, then a laughing dismissal of what she had said. Before he could deliver either Cassie had pocketed her first bite between her lips and was smiling at him.

'You should try the lamb,' she said casually. 'It's delicious.'

Wyatt knew that ignoring her accusation would lend

it too much importance, and forced himself to continue the discussion. 'There's some truth to what you say,' he responded carefully, watching her face. 'I've never treated a case quite like yours. It may be that no one has. Psychiatrically, I'm on unfamiliar ground, and that makes me uncomfortable. I didn't realise it was that obvious.'

She stabbed another piece of lamb with her fork and chewed it thoughtfully. 'Yesterday you asked me what I thought of you. Today, I'd like to know what you think of me.'

He laid his fork quietly on his plate and pushed his chair back from the table, regarding her steadily. 'I think you may have a future in psychiatry,' he responded grudgingly, his expression stiff and guarded. 'But I don't intend to submit as your first patient. I'm the one who's supposed to ask the questions here, remember?' There was a throaty huskiness in his voice she had never heard before, and she responded to it instantly.

'I can't help it,' she whispered in a response so rapid she had no time to mask its sincerity. 'I want to know everything about you.'

His face froze, and the barriers shot up on cue. 'When you're finished with your lunch, we'll get back to work. We've wasted too much time already.'

Cassie shivered at the sudden chill in his voice, then patted her lips delicately with her napkin. 'I'm finished,' she replied coolly. 'What's on this afternoon's schedule? Mountain climbing?'

'Nothing as easy as that. This afternoon we talk.'

He let her find her own way outside, then cupped her elbow in one hand and led her carefully around the back of the house, across rough, untended ground that quickly gave way to thick brush. 'There's just a small strip of this,' he told her when she hesitated. 'We'll come to a path soon, and the going will be easier.'

She moved forward without comment, lifting her feet high to clear the long, tangled grasses of late summer.

Wyatt glanced to his right occasionally, watching her as they walked.

There were times, he thought, when the blind had such dignity. They never looked down as they walked, as sighted people did, and the very fact that their faces remained lifted gave them a peculiar elegance. And their eyes were always quiet; never darting from side to side, busily absorbing all that was around them, but instead remained steadily fixed on whatever vision lay trapped in the darkness before them. With Cassie in particular, the serenity of her gaze made him think not of a blind person, but of someone looking at a point far in the distance; someone who could simply see farther than he could.

'Where are we going?' she asked suddenly, startling him out of his reverie.

'The path goes to the top of a hill behind the main house. Watch it—there's a piece of deadwood right in front of us.' He slowed her with his hand, guiding her carefully over the obstruction. 'The hill is flat on top, like a miniature butte,' he continued, 'and the scenery is spectacular.'

'I thought you said we wouldn't be climbing any mountains,' she reminded him petulantly, her legs complaining at the unaccustomed exercise.

'This is no mountain,' he chuckled. 'But it is the highest point in the county. You can see for miles in any direction.'

'*You* can, you mean.'

'You'll feel it, and I think you'll like it. It's a good place to talk. Better than some stuffy office on a day like today.'

They climbed on in silence, concentrating fully on the exertion required to manage the ever-steepening incline. Cassie tripped once, over a dead branch that protruded from the undergrowth on her side of the path, and his arm caught her around the waist securely and supported her while she regained her balance.

'Sorry,' he said quickly. 'I should have seen that.'

'Why so solicitous, Doctor?' she panted between breaths. 'I thought leading the blind around was breaking one of your cardinal rules.'

'Two reasons,' he answered, pulling her forward gently. 'One: we don't expect you to leave Windrow and start trail-blazing through the wilderness. That's not what we train you for. And two: I don't want you frustrated by any tests of physical endurance this afternoon. I want your mind clear, and relaxed, so you can concentrate.

After a few more steps, she stopped without warning, her body inclined slightly forward to compensate for the angle of their ascent, her lips parted at an unfamiliar sensation. 'We're there, aren't we?' she whispered. 'I can feel the wind on my face, like it's been blowing for hundreds of miles with nothing to stop it.'

'Just a few more steps . . .' he began, but she pulled away, scrambling upwards like a child who simply could not wait, stumbling, catching herself on her hands, finally topping the summit and standing triumphantly.

'It's fantastic!' she cried, and the wind threw her words back over her shoulder. 'What's in front of me?'

'Nothing. Nothing on any side. Just grass.'

She hesitated, then in one swift motion, unclasped the barrette that bound her hair and shook it out until the wind took it. It was pulled away from her head like a thousand dancing kite tails, whipping around her face to catch on her lashes, then blowing free again. She was no longer conscious of Wyatt's presence, or of her blindness, or of any of the hundred restrictions that had closed her off from the world for so many years. The wind and the space consumed her senses, infecting her with freedom, and she began to laugh, spinning where she stood, turning in tight circles with arms outstretched for balance.

At last she crumpled to the ground, flinging herself backward until she lay flat, facing the sky, panting with happy exhaustion. The sun touched her face in a thousand different ways, kissing the pink of flushed cheeks, dancing in mad sparks through the hair that flowed around her head like waves of light cresting. She felt the warmth of the sun suddenly blocked by his shadow, and lifted her chin to point at where she thought his eyes would be.

'I feel like I'm on top of the world,' she said softly, 'and there's nothing in my way.'

Wyatt frowned down at her, assessing her reaction, wondering how he could use it. She was no longer a twenty-five-year-old woman with years of darkness behind her; she was a child again—open, carefree, and infinitely vulnerable.

'When was the last time you felt like this?' he asked, kneeling beside her on the grass carpet, then reclining to face her on his side, supported by one elbow.

'When I could see,' she responded immediately, flinging her arms back over her head, catching the long grass between her fingers.

'And what do you see now?' he asked carefully.

She froze in place, her eyes narrowing against the brightness of the sun. 'What do you mean?'

'Pretend you can see,' he commanded. 'Close your eyes, imagine that you have your sight, and describe what you see.'

She chuckled nervously, then rolled on her side to face him, the motion bringing her body to within inches of his. 'Is this a game, or serious business?'

'Serious business,' he said sternly, quickly pulling himself away from her and up to a sitting position, wrapping his arms around his knees.

She followed his voice and rose to kneel next to him, reaching out with one hand to find his arm. He forced himself to remain immobile under her touch as her hand moved quickly up to touch the side of his face, hesitating as the short stubble of a day's beard prickled her fingers. 'I see you,' she said quietly, resting her hand on his shoulder.

'That's not sight,' he - said forcefully. 'That's imagination. What do you really see?'

'An angry man,' she said seriously.

Her jerked his shoulder away from her hand, leaving it suspended foolishly in mid-air. 'What do you see?' he demanded harshly, his voice rising over the wind.

'I told you!' she shouted back at him. 'I see you!'

'That's a lie! You're not trying! You don't want to see! You want to be blind!'

She dropped her hand and scrambled backward, astounded at how quickly he had changed, changing the world around him as well. Suddenly the gentle wind roared inside her ears; the hill was no longer the freedom of open space, but a formless void; and most frightening of all, the sun's quiet warmth had become a searing, oppressive heat, pressing down on her, confining her, making it difficult to breathe.

It's just stress, she told herself frantically, squeezing her eyes shut. It's not real. You can breathe; there's plenty of air. He's just making you mad, and you're reacting . . .

'What do you see?' His voice was loud, but strangely muffled, and colours assaulted her brain in a violent, unexpected swirl of yellow and orange.

It isn't real, it isn't real, she reassured herself with silent thoughts that trampled over one another in their urgency. Stop thinking about it. Think about the sky, blue sky, remember blue? You had a blue dress once . . .

'*What do you see?*' The voice was disembodied; hard, loud, terrifying; penetrating her reason, shredding it like a curtain, exposing the yellow and orange behind it.

She jumped to her feet, eyes so wide that the whites showed all around the brilliant blue irises, lips parted in horror. Wyatt leaped upright and stopped, paralysed by her expression, afraid to push her one step further on the path her mind had chosen. But he was driven now beyond controlling it; and the words left his mouth in a booming roar before he could consider stopping them. 'WHAT DO YOU SEE?'

She backed up slowly, her eyes fixed with terror on whatever image her mind had drawn, and her voice sounded parched, as if her throat had been seared by the picture in her brain. 'Fire,' she croaked. 'It's fire!' Then she spun away to flee the image and the voice, swallowing a scream, and her foot was only inches from the edge of the hill's flat summit when his arms finally lunged out to snatch her back.

He pulled her close to him, cradling her head on his chest, stroking her hair as she quivered wordlessly against him.

Gradually the fiery vision faded and her mind was blessedly black again. She stopped trembling then, and was fully conscious for the first time of his arms around her. She heard the distant thump of his heart in her ear, and pressed closer to the sound, like a motherless puppy seeking the reassurance of an alarm clock's ticking. There was an answering pull from his arms as he drew her closer.

'I lost it,' she murmured into his chest. 'I was so close to remembering; then I lost it.'

'It won't come all at once,' he said into her hair, tasting the strands with his lips. 'Only in pieces. Your mind is preparing you, bit by bit. It will all fit together eventually.'

The husky timbre of his voice raised the fine, silken hairs at the nape of her neck, and suddenly the faint musk of aftershave prickled her nostrils. The fragrance acted like a catalyst, startling her into an awareness of the nearness, and the intense maleness of the man who held her. Suddenly he was not Dr Wyatt Field, and she was not Cassandra Winters. They had no identity at all. They were simply man and woman; no, more basic even than that. Male animal and female animal; elemental, almost primeval, so ancient were the thundering sensations that passed between them.

Neither moved, yet the awesome forces within their bodies made them catch their breath together, and hold it, until it seemed to each that the earth beneath their feet had begun to tremble. And then, without warning, without conscious intent, Cassie stirred against him.

Wyatt's arms tightened in a sudden convulsion to feel the body in his embrace change so subtly, yet so completely within the space of a single heartbeat. The child nestling close for comfort had abruptly become a woman, moulding her body to his, demanding with the insidious pressure of hip and breast a fulfilment of the desire that drove it. His eyes flew wide at the artful touch of pelvis and thigh, then his own body responded with an instinctive swiftness he was powerless to prevent, and the chain of passion was begun.

Her back arched against the broad forearm that pressed against it, and her head fell back, exposing her throat in an animal's gesture of submission. She felt the heat of his breath fall on her neck, and knew with an instinct that belied her inexperience that his eyes were narrowed, touching the firm, straining swells that tightened against the low neck of her blouse. There was a feathery brush as a lock of his hair touched the hollow of her throat, then a slow, voluptuous shudder passed through her body, and she laced fingers behind his neck to pull his head down.

For the briefest of moments, the cords in his neck stood out as he resisted the pull of her hands, then the resistance faltered, and the moist heat of his lips burned the slope of one breast before he shuddered violently and pushed her from him.

'No!' he roared, and there was nothing human in the sound of his voice. It was the mystified bellow of a wounded animal; the angry outcry of a wild beast denied its prey; the savage scream of the lion that sends natives scurrying for the safety of their fires in the darkness of a jungle night. Forever afterwards, whenever she heard his voice in anger, Cassie would remember this moment, and think of the call of a lion in darkness, and tremble. She staggered backward away from the sound, suddenly chilled and fearful.

Wyatt stood away from her, his arms held stiffly at his sides, his chest heaving with each ragged breath. His lips were parted over clenched teeth, his eyes hooded to narrow slits of blue light that watched her warily. When his gaze dropped to touch on the rapid rise and fall of the twin mounds beneath her blouse, he jerked his head up savagely and focused on the blank, troubled eyes that seemed to accuse him.

'I'm sorry,' he whispered hoarsely, the unaccustomed words sticking in his throat.

'You should be,' she said shakily, sucking in her lower lip like a petulant child. 'You never finish anything you start!'

'Cassie,' the word was pulled from his lips in an agonised hiss. 'You don't understand. You don't understand anything.'

Suddenly her face cleared, and there was a bright, calculating flash from her eyes. 'Yes I do,' she said slowly. 'I understand that you want me.' The statement was eloquently simple, and Wyatt dropped his chin to his chest in a silent, quaking admission that she could not see.

Then he raised his head and his features tightened with an ugly resolve. 'I've wanted many women in my life,' he growled, forcing the lie between his teeth, then embellishing it. 'You're no different from a hundred others.'

He watched disbelief, then dismay creep across her face in a shadow of pain, and knew that she believed him. 'Nothing ever stood in the way of taking a woman I wanted,' he continued slowly, 'but this time something does. I can't be your doctor and your lover both, so I've chosen one. The most important one. It wasn't even a difficult choice. Having one less woman isn't going to affect the rest of my life.'

He nearly choked on the words, forcing himself to watch as emotion slid from her face, leaving it blank and empty. He fought the impulse to fall to his knees before her, to bury his face in her stomach and let the tide wash over them, drowning them both; and stood quietly instead, waiting.

She closed her eyes and stood rigidly straight, letting his words lash her like a physical beating, hearing them over and over again in her mind. Part of him ached to see her stand there and take it; but another part, the part of self he guarded jealously from the encroachment of emotion, fed on her anguish and wanted to use it against her. 'I know you're feeling all sorts of things you've never felt before,' he said blithely. 'You're going through the sexual awakening most young women experience in their teens. But I'm not where you are, Cassie.' He forced out a disdainful chuckle. 'I've been there already; a very long time ago. There's nothing you can give me that a dozen other women haven't given before. Nothing. Do you understand?'

She nodded her head once in a shallow dip, and her lower lip quivered.

Don't feel badly about it,' he said, and could hardly believe that he had managed to sound so casual while his heart hammered against the wall of his chest, and every muscle in his body screamed to reach out to her. 'It's nothing to be ashamed of. One day you'll look back on it and laugh.'

He squeezed his eyes shut at the sheer inanity of his words; at what must be the obvious transparency of his lies; but her lips trembled in a weak, fluttering smile as she accepted them without question.

'Shall we go back now?' he asked with artificial brightness, and she nodded her answer in a stoic silence that wrenched at his heart.

Wyatt worried through every silent step on their walk back to the main house, stealing apprehensive glances at Cassie whenever she was distracted by the terrain. She moved with leaden resignation, sinking deeper and deeper into a depression that would prove invincible, unless he could find a way to check it soon. In solving one problem, he had created another for this withdrawal into apathy would close her mind against probing every bit as effectively as her passion had.

'Show me your room,' he said impulsively as they entered the building, and she nodded without comment and led the way up the broad staircase.

'I want you to relax, now,' he commanded gently, closing the door behind them. 'Lie down. Close your eyes.'

She turned her head uncertainly towards the bed, wanting desperately to sink into the comfort of its softness, to give in to the exhaustion that had crept up on her so quickly, to sleep for days and days; perhaps forever.

Wyatt saw the heavily-lidded eyes, and knew her mind was anticipating the escape of sleep in a classic symptom of acute depression. And that he knew how to handle.

'I'm just going to sit with you for a while. That's all.'

He took a seat in the room's only occasional chair and plunked his feet noisily on the ottoman. His head bobbed in silent approval as she moved slowly towards the bed, then he passed a hand over his eyes, fighting the need to sleep away the day's emotional strain, forcing lightness into his voice.

'You liked Dr Franklin, didn't you?' he asked.

She lowered herself stiffly to sit on the edge of the bed, and nodded silently.

'He has a lovely home a few miles from here, and a lovely wife—Katy. I think you'd enjoy her. Would you like to have dinner with them Friday night, just to get away from all this for a while?'

He watched her face carefully, noting the slow blinks, the almost glazed appearance of her eyes. She nodded again, hesitantly, but still said nothing. Her hands pressed deep into the bed at her sides, and her fingers worked nervously at the threads of the chenille spread.

'Dr Franklin and I have worked together for years,' he continued casually, 'and we have a good relationship.

So good, in fact, that at one time he harboured a secret fantasy about matching me with his daughter.'

Her eyes seemed to focus slightly, and she frowned a little.

'He doesn't know I know this, of course,' he said confidentially, 'and I would never tell him, but his attempts at matchmaking were pretty obvious. He did everything but pick me up off the ground and throw me at her.'

A smile touched the corners of her mouth, and he closed his eyes briefly in relief. He was drawing her out slowly, cautiously, teasing her with conversation that would pull her thoughts away from what had happened on the hill.

'I take it it wasn't a perfect match,' she said quietly, and he drew a deep breath of satisfaction to hear her speak.

'Hardly,' he chuckled. 'Marianne could barely tolerate me. She married an oil rigger, or some such thing, and escaped her father's designs just as quickly as she could.'

Cassie's lips moved into a genuine smile at the thought of someone turning *him* down, then she yawned in the first gesture of honest relaxation. 'I'm tired,' she said simply. 'I'd like to go to sleep.'

'In a minute,' he said impatiently. 'But first I want to talk about what you saw up on the hill. Can you do that?'

She frowned and pressed the fingers of one hand to her forehead. 'There isn't much to talk about. I saw fire, and it frightened me. That's all.'

'But it doesn't frighten you now? Remembering it?'

'No, not really. It's hazy now, like a movie I saw a long time ago.'

He nodded. 'Just like the piano piece. Once you've recalled it, the fear vanishes. Do you understand that? The fear of the memory is worse than the memory itself.' He leaned forward in his chair, bracing his arms on his knees, his gaze strangely intense. 'It would be easier, Cassie, if you could reconstruct the accident consciously. Easier on you. Forcing the subconscious to remember against the conscious will is always more difficult, and more draining. It's like living through it again, instead of simply recalling it. Will you try to remember?'

She nodded grimly, tensing.

'All right then. The fire was obviously related to the accident; therefore we have to assume that the car burned. And you saw it.' He hesitated intentionally, scanning her face for any reaction, but it remained composed and indifferent. His voice took on a lulling, soothing quality. 'If you saw your mother trapped in a burning car, unable to help her, it would have been an almost unbearable trauma. Frustration, anger, and above all, guilt—would all work together to create a mental block. Think now. Can you recall anything like that?'

She closed her eyes tightly, concentrating all her energy in a desperate effort to remember, then finally shrugged. 'I'm sorry. Nothing.'

He took a deep breath to prepare himself, then leaped up out of his chair and allowed his voice to explode over her head. 'Grow up, dammit!' he shouted, and she jerked to attention, her eyes wide and startled. His tone lowered to a sinister drawl, and contempt laced his words. 'You expect an adult man to take you seriously?' he sneered. 'You're just a child, hiding in a woman's body, hiding from the memory that could make you whole! You're only half a woman, Cassie Winters. Maybe even less than that.'

She gasped in shocked disbelief at the suddenness and intensity of his attack, and her mouth remained open while her cheeks flushed a bright scarlet. 'Get out!' she shrilled finally, and one side of Wyatt's mouth turned up in a bitter, satisfied smile.

'Gladly,' he said softly, and slammed the door behind him. He sagged against the wall on the other side, and grinned to hear the dull, muffled thuds of a tiny fist being repeatedly slammed into a pillow. 'Good, Cassie,' he whispered shakily. 'Good for you.'

CHAPTER EIGHT

THE moment Cassie slid into her chair opposite him at the table that night, she knew he had changed. A dozen senses warned her before he said a word, and when he did speak, his voice confirmed it. There was a new edge to it; a hard, cold edge, like the steel of an unused blade. He rebuffed her first attempt at casual conversation with an impatient reminder that their meeting was in no way a social one.

'We've cracked the door,' he said coldly. 'We've seen the piano piece, and the fire, and we're going to keep pushing until we see the rest.'

There was no promise in his voice, only an open threat; and Cassie shivered with the very unpleasant sensation of having become, in the small space of a few hours, the enemy.

'You're different,' she remarked quietly.

'No, I'm not,' he lied, containing with a tremendous effort of will the impulse to touch the soft swell of her cheek. 'We've just been playing up to now; taking it slow, and easy.'

'I see,' she said evenly, lifting one side of her mouth in bitter resignation. 'But now the party's over; is that it?'

He tightened the fingers of one hand into a white fist. 'Yes. The party's over,' he said flatly.

The meal was stiff with formalities and short, sharp responses to any question she dared ask. At its end, her final query was timid and uncertain. 'May we walk tonight?'

'Do whatever you like,' he replied indifferently. 'I'm going home.'

His mood had not altered by the next morning; if anything, it was even more intense. After the first hour, Cassie felt like a helpless bystander to a terrible battle between two awesome, equal forces: the power of Wyatt Field's determination; and the power of her own mind. There was no trace of the man who had touched her with trembling, troubled passion by the creek; no remnant of the man who had held her in comforting arms up on the hill; and his replacement terrified her. His assignment to force her memory, to force her to see, became an obsessive, unholy crusade, and without conscious intent, her mind began to close against him.

Through the next few days he hammered at her consciousness relentlessly, trying to coax memory from her in rare periods of quiet, searching conversation; then reverting abruptly to harsh, shotgun interrogation that left her bewildered and wary. But her mind remained frustratingly blank. She wanted to remember; she tried desperately to remember; the fear at incurring his wrath becoming every bit as great as the fear of never seeing again. She didn't need to see his face to know that when she said, 'I don't remember,' it darkened and became tight with accusation. But no matter how earnest her efforts, no matter how merciless his questions, the past remained buried, and the world remained black.

There were moments when she thought she could sense an underlying tenderness in his manner; moments when his desperation was so keen that she became fleetingly aware that his battle was more personal than he might admit. But those moments became fewer and farther between as her spirit wilted under the constant emotional strain. She felt herself growing mentally weaker, felt her self-control slipping, and developed an uncharacteristic tendency to cry herself to sleep.

'We're not getting anywhere!' she complained bitterly one morning, close to tears after an especially cruel round of questions. He was unusually quiet, and she reached out without thinking to touch his arm, a gesture she had not dared make for days. She thought she sensed a slight loosening of taut muscles under her fingers, but then he picked up her hand and removed it from his arm with a contempt that bordered on distaste.

'But then we're not finished yet,' he said coldly, and she shrank in her chair, shaken by his obvious contempt.

Wyatt's supervision was so constant that she was denied even the comfort of Maggie's company and understanding, and this she missed most of all. Her days began and ended in his presence, until it seemed that he was the fulcrum around which her life revolved; a perverted, sadistic centre to an existence that made no allowances, and forgave no errors.

'Stop!' he would shout as she moved one foot to step down from a kerb, and she would bring her other foot forward for balance, and remain obediently still. His fingers would press into the flesh of her arm as he jerked her backwards up on to the kerb. 'I told you to stop!' he would hiss into her ear.

'I did stop!' she would protest, but his answer was always the same.

'Not fast enough! You took another step! Some day your life may depend on how quickly you react to the warning of a sighted person. The next time you hear someone say stop, *stop*!'

The days were a peculiar combination of exercises designed to help her function as a blind person, and furious, intense attempts to force her to remember, and to see. As they wore on, her confidence faltered under the barrage of his criticism, and she longed only for those dark moments of solitude in her room each night, when she was blessedly free of Wyatt Field. As the end of the first week drew near, she became uneasy with the sensation of a clock somewhere ticking ominously down.

She waited sullenly at the breakfast table Friday morning, steeling herself for the rigours of yet another day in an endless succession of days under his cruel tutelage. Only her pride sustained her, and even that was showing signs of wear in the forced lift of her chin, the exaggerated set of her shoulders as she heard him approach the table.

'Good morning, Cassie.'

Her nod was almost imperceptible.

'Shall we begin by talking about your mother again, or your father?'

'Neither. I don't feel like talking today, and that's one thing that even you can't force me to do.' Her voice sounded childishly petulant, even to her.

'Fine,' he responded lightly, apparently unconcerned with her determination not to co-operate. 'There are other things we can do if you choose not to talk. The verbal duels were getting tiresome, anyway.'

His statement had the ring of a threat, and she frowned suspiciously.

His lips curved into a grudging smile as he watched her face, noting as he had so often in the past few days the way shadows flitted across her features with the pattern of her thoughts, revealing more than she knew. He reached across the table to touch her hand in the first gentle physical gesture he had made in days. The sensation was so startling that she jerked her fingers away without thinking.

'Sorry,' he said casually. 'You're a little jumpy this morning, aren't you?'

'I spend all my waking hours with a sadist,' she retorted hotly. 'You'd be jumpy, too. Thank God it's half over.'

His smile was thin and forced. 'You might as well thank God you're going to stay blind, if you're talking about your two weeks with me.'

'So far my time with you hasn't been very productive,' she said bitterly. 'Or hadn't you noticed? I'm still blind, Dr Field.'

'I noticed,' he replied steadily, ignoring her sarcasm. 'I never said it would be easy, or fast; but you *will* remember, Cassie. And you *will* see.'

There was an ugly stubbornness in his tone; an absolute refusal to accept defeat, and she narrowed her eyes suspiciously. 'I'm the ultimate challenge, aren't I?' she accused him. 'Your key to fame and fortune. The case that will set precedents; put your name in all the textbooks; the case of a lifetime.'

'You might say that,' he answered softly.

'Well then, let's get on with it,' she said bitterly, pushing herself away from the table. 'Far be it from me to stand in your way. Where to?'

He stared deeply into the angry eyes that refused to see his, and sorrow crossed his face in a dark shadow. 'Lead us to the gymnasium,' he said quietly, and she shrugged in indifference, and rose from her chair.

The morning air was sharp with the promise of an early fall, and Cassie felt the feeble warmth of a sun partially obscured by haze. 'Is it fog, or just clouds?' she asked as she led the way down the circular walk towards the gymnasium building.

'You tell me.'

He would never answer a question if he thought she could answer it herself, and the practice was increasingly irritating. 'All right!' she snapped. 'It's not fog because there's no moisture in the air, and the morning is too cool for haze. That leaves two possibilities: pollution, or clouds.'

'Do you smell pollution?'

She inhaled deeply, then smiled involuntarily as her mind was assaulted with a surge of fragrances she had never encountered in the city. 'Of course not,' she relented, buoyed slightly by the crisp, bracing quality of morning air in the country. 'Although there was a car here a short time ago. You can still smell the exhaust.'

As if on cue, Wyatt's ears heard the distant thump of a car door closing in the lot behind the medical building, and he shook his head in grudging admiration. The smell of exhaust had completely eluded him.

'And by the way, the clouds are cirrus—high-flying.'

Wyatt tipped his head to confirm her statement, and nodded in silent satisfaction. Her perception, and her powers of deduction, continued to improve at an encouraging rate.

'It's supposed to clear later today,' he murmured absently. 'Maybe by the time we're finished in the gym.'

Her steps faltered only slightly. His command to lead him to the gymnasium had come as no surprise. At least once a day he demanded that she find one building or another, until now she felt she could easily locate any building on campus. 'I could find these buildings with my eyes closed,' she had said in jest the other day, but if her remark had prompted a smile, he had given no indication of it. But now it appeared they were finally to enter one, and she shuddered to think what physical rigours he might have planned for their time in the gymnasium.

She turned confidently to the right when her feet hit the rectangle where the concrete walk abruptly dipped to dirt, and followed the path at a slower gait until she sensed the squat building looming before her.

'Do you want to go inside?' she asked timidly.

'Yes.'

The door was a heavy metal affair with a long, metal bar that yielded when she pushed inward. As the door thumped shut behind them, she cocked her head, assimilating the new sounds and smells in the unfamiliar surroundings.

'Blind people play basketball?' she asked in wonder, separating the noises a ball made as it was bounced on a hardwood floor, and then against a suspended backboard.

'They do. There's a beeper on the rim of the basket. Some of our students leave here with a record-breaking accuracy from the free-throw line. The door to the gym itself is right in front of you.'

She started to move obediently forward.

'No. We won't go into the gym today. I just wanted you to know where it was.'

She stopped suddenly, aware of what he had planned. 'The swimming pool?' she asked fearfully.

He nodded and smiled, then immediately berated himself for forgetting, as he caught himself doing often, that Cassie could not see the movement of his head. 'Yes. The swimming pool.'

She knew he would expect her to find the pool herself, so didn't bother to wait for him to verbalise the command. She turned left reluctantly, and followed the sharp, pervasive scent of chlorine. She hugged the right-hand wall, turned at the first corridor she came to, and hesitated when her hand brushed the hinges of a heavy door.

'This is it,' she said softly.

'Then let's go in.'

She entered what felt like a cavernous room, sensing an enormous, threatening body of water directly ahead and to her left. The door closed behind them with a finality that echoed in the hollow chamber, and she jumped.

'There's a door directly on your right,' he said mechanically. 'Straight ahead as you enter is a bank of lockers. You'll find your name in braille on a plate at eye level on one of them. Inside the locker is a suit that will fit you, or a couple of suits to try if Maggie wasn't sure of your size. I'll be waiting right here, and don't be long. We only have the pool for two hours this morning.'

'Will you be swimming, too?'

'Yes. But I'll be changed and back out here before you find your locker. Don't keep me waiting.'

He gave her a gentle push on the back, and she dragged her feet across the tiny mosaic tiles until a door opened under her hands. She closed it behind her and leaned back against it, breathing deeply to calm her nerves. She wasn't even sure she remembered how to swim, as her mind raced back to playful afternoons in the family pool when she was a child. Was it like riding a bicycle? Something your body remembered? Even after nearly twenty years?

She trembled as she started to cross the narrow room,

her arms stretched out at head-level in front of her. Her mouth twisted in a bitter smile when she realised she had unconsciously broken the first rule she had learned at Windrow, about keeping her hands at waist level. So what if I look like a blind person, she thought resentfully. He's not here to see, or to shout. The hell with him. Her shin cracked against the unyielding edge of something hard and wooden, and she doubled over with a gasp to rub at the pain, cursing under her breath. She groped with her hands until she identified a wooden bench, confirming that it had a high back, like the benches in Central Park. She could have avoided the obstacle if only her arms had not been held so high. Even out of his sight, his lessons haunted her, punishing her when she ignored them.

Her lips tightened in anger as she circuited the bench and felt for the face of the lockers. Hers was the third from the left, and though she found it quickly, her fingers returned to linger on other nameplates, discerning the unfamiliar names of fellow students now residing in the dormitory. They had only been vague shadows in her mind before: faceless people whose existence she had never really considered. But now, with the reality of their names beneath her trembling fingers, she felt the elation of discovery. In the space of an instant, she was not alone anymore. Not the only blind person in a universe of sight. There were others like her. They existed; they were real; and they had names.

Susan Beckman. Who was she? Was she old, or young? And Elaine Alistair. How about her? How was she blinded? Was she bitter, or resigned? Was she the woman whose face went through the windshield? The one Dr Field had talked about?

'Hey! Are you coming?' There was a sharp rap on the door, and she turned to the sound.

'In a few minutes!' she called out, strangely giddy with her discovery.

She felt inside her locker for the limp shape of a swimming suit, then began to shed her clothes quickly.

Alone in the darkness for eighteen years, within seconds she had found kindred spirits in an empty locker room. People who shared her fears and her uncertainties; people linked with her by a bond stronger than any relationship she had ever experienced; and her mind rejoiced to find fellowship.

The enormity of her father's unintentional cruelty registered for only a moment, then she shrugged it away with a satisfied sigh. He had isolated her not only from the world of the sighted, but from the world of the blind, as well. She had not realised until this moment how crushing that deprivation had been. But it was over. She forgave him instantly, and jerked on the one-piece tank suit she had found hanging in her locker.

Without sight to evaluate and question her appearance, she was totally unselfconscious about appearing before Dr Field in a suit so starkly simple that it accentuated every line of her body. It was a body she had never seen, and she was as innocently immodest about it as a child would be.

Still buoyed by the revelation that she was no longer the only blind person in the world, she stepped out of the locker room smiling, supported by the presence of people she had never met, whose names she would never forget. Susan Beckman. Elaine Alistair. Silent friends. Dr Field didn't seem nearly as intimidating now, and whatever tasks he set would be easier. After all, Susan had been through it; and Elaine; and if they could manage, she would too.

Wyatt's head dropped back on his shoulders when he saw her, and his eyes narrowed. He would berate himself later for failing to notice, in those first few seconds, the serene radiance of her expression; but like a man afflicted with tunnel vision, his awareness was completely consumed by the swells and dips of a body his mind had never dared imagine. That she was totally unaware of her beauty made him feel strangely guilty for noticing it.

Cassie stood quietly by the door, her long hair shifting slightly as she tipped her head first one way, then the other, trying to determine where he stood. There was a new confidence in her stature, and in the steady, patient gaze of remarkable blue eyes that seemed to lock on to his, holding him captive.

Wyatt dropped his chin to his chest and took a deep breath.

'What took you so long?' he asked gruffly, and Cassie heard the break in his voice that usually indicated impatience.

'I was making friends,' she responded mysteriously.

And then, finally, he noticed the expression that heralded a monumental transformation, and he caught his breath in his throat, stunned by the innocent rapture on her face.

He turned abruptly from her without saying a word, and dove into the turquoise water, his body cutting through the still surface so cleanly that it barely rippled. He stayed under for nearly a full minute, until he could feel the prickling fire in his lungs; until his entire body was forced to focus on the simple demands of survival, excluding everything else. Then he shot upward like a bullet, feeling strangely cleansed.

Cassie had moved closer to the edge of the pool, her toes curled over the smooth tile lip; and jumped back with a short, delighted squeal when the force of his surfacing splashed her. The hesitation her fear had created earlier was totally absent, and for a moment, Wyatt was afraid she would plunge in heedlessly, before he had a chance to instruct her.

'Can you swim?' he asked from beneath her as he trod water.

'I don't know!' she answered happily.

'Then turn left and walk to the corner of the pool. That's the shallow end. We'll start there.'

He submerged briefly under the rope of floats that divided the pool, following her progress along the side until he met her at the end.

'There are four steps into the water,' he told her. 'Semi-circular.'

She felt for the steps carefully with her feet, descending until the cool water lapped at her waist, pausing with her arms held out, shivering in delight. 'I can't do this,' she laughed, closing her eyes. 'I have to get wet all at once.' Then without warning, she flung herself forward and bellyflopped next to him, rolling the water until his feet were lifted off the pool floor.

She came up in a flying spray, like a nymph bursting forth from a fountain, finding her footing and shaking long, blonde strands away from her face. 'This is wonderful!' she cried.

Wyatt stood motionless, mesmerised by the exhilaration of her reaction. She began a slow, uncertain crawl across the width of the pool, turning when her fingertips grazed the tile, ploughing back towards him through the water, her strokes becoming longer and more sure.

His muscles rippled with almost unbearable tension when her fingers brushed against his stomach, but he stood rigidly immobile.

'Guess what!' she laughed, leaping to an upright position in front of him. 'I can swim!'

That something unexpected had happened in the locker room, something that had altered her perception of herself, was patently obvious. Her attitude towards him had changed, and the change had made her almost casually confident. His features tightened into a scowl of frustration, and he felt an angry pulse quicken in his throat.

'What happened in there?' he demanded, grasping her shoulders and holding her still.

She opened her mouth and drew in a great breath, then closed it again and held the breath in, her eyes busy with excitement. 'It's hard to explain,' she blurted with her exhale. 'Except that everything seems ... different. Better.'

'I can see that,' he said drily, trying to restrain her

bobbing motions as she bounced up and down, entranced with the buoyancy the water gave her. 'But what happened? Specifically.'

She grinned with her secret, trying to decide whether saying it aloud would lessen its effect. 'It was the nameplates on the lockers,' she said in a rush. 'They have *names*. It made them real!' She hesitated and pressed her lips together in sudden sobriety. 'For eighteen years,' she said seriously, 'I've been the only blind person in a world where everyone else could see. No one was going through what I was; no one could understand my problems, or my fears, or how damn *hard* everything was. And now, all of a sudden, I have company!'

A smile barely touched her lips before it exploded into an uncontrollable giggle. Her hands fluttered under the water, restricted by his grasp on her shoulders, trying desperately to release through physical motion the exaltation she felt.

He shook her slightly in frustration, wondering how to recapture the hostility he would channel to use against her mind's stubborn refusal to see, and sensed sadly that he may have lost his chance forever. Happy people do not examine their subconscious, or search their memory for skeletons. They wallow in the contentment of the moment, asking for nothing more. It was the most painful part of his job, knowing that only when his patients were engaged in a struggle would they make progress. Cassie was obviously too pleased with herself and life in general at the moment to strive to change anything. She was almost invulnerable.

His shoulders sagged in despair, and although he was not aware of the long sigh he emitted, Cassie heard it. Suddenly he was no longer the invincible Dr Field, but merely a man, subject to the emotions and frustrations common to all men. It was like a gift, to find the robot human after all. A gift in celebration of her own lightness of heart; and she could no longer suppress the instinctive expression of joy.

She sank quickly from his grasp beneath the water, and Wyatt felt a sharp jerk on his ankle as her hand groped and pulled his feet out from under him. He went over backwards and swallowed the bitter taste of chlorine with a mouth opened in surprise, then broke the surface to a mad deluge of water as she moved her arms in wild pinwheels, splashing him mercilessly.

'What the hell ...?' He stood stupidly under the onslaught, without the first notion of how to respond to such atypical behaviour, until his voice provided the target for handfuls of water she flung merrily into his face, then his response came automatically. Without a single conscious thought of what he was doing, or whether or not it was appropriate, he began to sweep huge waves of water over her head, and felt not the slightest remorse as she backed away, laughing, covering her face with her hands in a useless effort to protect herself. For a moment at least, they were two children playing in a pool, freed from the cumbersome responsibilities of adulthood, and laughter bounced off the tile walls of the bright, sterile room.

When the first frenzy of activity faded, the realisation of who he was, and what he was doing, struck Wyatt with unforgiving clarity, and he stilled immediately.

Cassie's laughter stopped simultaneously with his as she sensed an abrupt change of mood, and they stood facing each other in the pool, breathing hard. Wyatt heard the unnatural sound of his own laughter still echoing in the air, and frowned suddenly.

'That's enough swimming for today,' he said brusquely, moving to walk towards the side of the pool.

'Why?' she protested, pushing forward to follow in his wake, reaching out until her hand found his forearm and closed around it. 'You said we had the pool for two hours. It can't be time yet.'

His eyes lowered as she rose from the water in front of him, blocking his way. The water sheeted off her shoulders and breasts as she stood, and sparkling droplets clung to the ends of her lashes as she frowned up into his face.

'Because,' he said uncertainly, 'this isn't accomplishing anything.'

She blew out her cheeks in exasperation and shot water into his face with the swipe of an open hand. 'Does *everything* have to accomplish some clinical purpose? Don't you ever make time for fun?'

'Only on my time, not yours,' he said sternly. 'Fun isn't what you're paying for.'

'You're obsessed with giving me my money's worth, you know that?' she said sharply. 'And what was swimming supposed to accomplish anyway?'

He frowned down at her, holding his arms tightly at his sides. 'Most blind people are terrified of the water at first,' he explained slowly. 'Overcoming that fear increases their trust in me, and eventually, in themselves. You obviously have no fear to overcome.'

She smiled suddenly, and placed both hands lightly on his shoulders. 'You should be pleased, then. It's one lesson you won't have to dwell on. I already trust you, and myself.'

His concentration narrowed dangerously to the two parts of his body under her hands, and he tried to back away from her. Her fingers simply tightened on his shoulders and she let the water lift her as she was pulled along, laughing as if it were all a game. Within a few steps he backed into the solid side of the pool, and her floating momentum brought her face into immediate and unexpected contact with his chest. She stood quickly, her smile faltering in the awkward silence. The ripples created by their passing gradually ebbed, and the gentle splashing against their immobile bodies slowed until they stood in a silence broken only by the separate sounds of their breathing.

With her lips parted, responding to a need as deep and demanding as anything she had ever felt, she moved her hands up to his cheeks, memorising the curves and the hollows there with her fingers. She felt his jaw clench and his neck stiffen, and explored the muscular column more insistently with one hand while the other wandered through the dark tangle of his hair.

'I'm only seeing you,' she said softly. 'You're supposed to be used to this, remember?'

Her hands slid in unison down the smooth slope of his shoulders, pressing lightly against the swell of biceps contracted in urgent tension, meeting eventually in the centre of his chest. His lids dropped like blinds to half-mast, partially concealing the flaming smoke of eyes gone suddenly dark, and his lips parted helplessly to draw in air without revealing by sound the intensity of his reaction to her touch.

She found the soft matt of damp hair on his chest and twisted it around her fingers, and the slightly painful tug as her hands moved on, pulling the hairs, concentrated his awareness to that part of his body with an explosion of sensuality. He tipped his head back slightly to bring her face into focus, and recoiled to find her eyes wide, apparently focused directly on his. He was as powerless to pull away as he would have been to stop breathing. No matter how urgently his mind screamed a silent warning to escape the touch of her hands, his body stubbornly refused to move away from the electricity of her fingertips. He squeezed his eyes tightly shut, pressed his hands to his sides against the pull of the water, and concentrated the remaining vestiges of his will against making his own physical response.

Cassie was enraptured by the feel of his body under her hands. It started as an instinctive need to reach out and touch him; developed as her hands explored to a curious wonder at the shape and the feel of a man's body; and then abruptly changed into something else altogether as her sensitive fingers recorded the involuntary response of his quivering muscles.

She heard him catch his breath and hold it when her hands descended to his chest, and felt the answering throb swell from her chest and travel to every pulse point in her body, until her fingertips felt huge, tingling with a cadenced beat like ten tiny drums. The sensation was extraordinary, and totally unfamiliar; this coursing heat that exploded in her stomach and travelled upward through her body, defying gravity, pressing on her chest, making it difficult to breathe. Her lips parted automatically to increase the intake of air, and the furious need to be touched by him burned like a raging fire, consuming her from the inside.

When the tight lace of his stomach muscles jumped inward away from her hands, her legs lost their ability to hold her erect, and she sagged forward slightly. Her thigh pressed against his beneath the water, and Wyatt felt the shock shoot upward from his leg, through his chest and into his arm, forcing it away from his side, guiding his hand to the white slope of her shoulder in a tentative touch his mind had never engineered. She shuddered when his fingers made contact, and the skin beneath them quivered as they traced a line from her shoulder to the slope of her breast, down to the hard point that pressed out against the thin fabric of her suit. She gasped weakly with the sudden burst of sensation, her ribs thrusting forward against the ridges of his stomach in an involuntary response.

She felt his wet hair brush her chin as his head bent to that shadowy line where suit met skin, and then it felt like her breasts were swelling, tightening against the confines of fabric, threatening to spill out over the top to meet his mouth. A startled sound flew up from her chest and escaped her lips, and she heard its harsh echo from somewhere inside her head. Her back arched and the full length of her body forced the water from between them as she pressed against him, trembling as she felt the answering throb of his heart through his hands, his mouth, and the rigid rock of the thighs that met hers. Then his fingers slipped into the tangled wetness on either side of her head, and he lowered his face slowly to hers, so that she felt the warm rush of his ragged breath long before his mouth claimed hers. The quivering movements of his lips hardened with an urgent pressure as his hands dropped to her waist beneath the water and jerked her body against him; then his tongue parted her lips under his with one darting touch, and an electric thrill flowed through her body with wave after wave of almost unbearable anticipation.

With one swift, desperate motion, she shrugged out of one strap of the tank suit and felt the unutterable pleasure of bare breast pressing against the hardness of his chest. He sprang back from her as if he had been burned, his eyes wide and disbelieving as he stared at the smooth white globe that seemed to float on the water's surface.

'What are you doing?' he demanded hoarsely, trying to hold her at arms' length while she struggled to push herself against him again.

Her eyebrows twitched in confusion and she shrugged. The movement lifted the exposed breast briefly from the water, then let it splash gently back down into its liquid cradle.

His fingers felt thick and awkward as he reached out quickly and slid the strap back up her arm, covering her body as if the sight had been offensive.

A quick, startled breath flew into her lungs when the fabric's cold elasticity flattened against the hard point of her breast, then her features sagged in misery. 'I don't understand,' she whispered between breaths. 'Am I ugly?'

He threw his head back and closed his eyes, and the cords of his neck stood out in sharp relief. 'God, no,' he murmured, trying to control the shudders racking his body, trying to relax the painful tightness of the muscles in his stomach. He felt the feather-light brush of fingers fluttering at his chest, and caught her hand and held it away from his body.

'Other people use the pool,' came the throaty reprimand. 'We could be interrupted at any time.'

'Aren't they all blind?' she asked practically, moving sinuously towards him.

He escaped her by sliding sideways along the edge of the pool, amazed to find his legs capable of any motion whatsoever. 'The staff isn't blind!' he snapped.

She stopped suddenly, and a slow smile spread across her face at the simplicity of the solution. 'Then let's go somewhere else,' she whispered.

'Cassie!' he shouted in frustration, and she started, recalling another time when she had heard his voice distorted by the rage of thwarted passion. He was the lion again, and she was the prey, trembling before the awesome force of his anger.

He glanced at her once through the distorted red haze of total frustration, then dove for the left side of the pool and pulled himself up by the edge. He stood motionless above her, saying nothing, and the silence was broken only by the sound of water dripping from his body and smacking the tiles beneath his feet.

'Come on out,' he ordered finally, his voice low and controlled. 'It's time for lunch. I'll meet you outside the building in ten minutes.'

She stood quietly for a moment until the reverberations of his voice had died away, listening for the soft thump of the men's locker room door closing behind him; then she sighed shakily and made her way to the edge of the pool and climbed out.

CHAPTER NINE

CASSIE dressed quickly, driven by a nervous anxiety that trembled in fingers grown suddenly awkward and fumbling. She was filled with the wary anticipation of a trainer holding a wild animal on a short leash, never completely certain that the beast will not turn and attack without warning.

She approached the building's outside door, then paused with her hand stretched towards it, breathing deeply, wondering at what she would find on the other side.

She was as certain of her own feelings as she was that the world was black, but his remained a mystery. Experience had not equipped her to divine the motivations of men, and she knew only one thing: the limits of their shattering clashes of body and will had been reached; the rage of their passion had gone beyond control; and the issue would have to be faced squarely and dealt with. He would demand that, and she was powerless to stop him.

She squared her shoulders and pushed through the door, and walked out into the sunlight to meet her future.

Wyatt was braced against the wall just outside the door, his arms crossed over his chest, holding the breath he had caught at the first click of the latch. Every muscle was tensed in agonising anticipation, for he knew as surely as she did that what passed between them in the next few moments would determine the course of their relationship, and her sight hung in the balance. There was a twisting pain in his chest as he gazed at the long, wet tangle of blonde framing a face still flushed a delicate pink, then he tightened his features and clenched his jaw, and waited.

She turned and smiled slowly at the place where he was standing, then silently extended one hand. He swallowed against the dryness in his throat, and eyed her outstretched hand warily.

'Come on,' she said with forced lightness, postponing the inevitable confrontation. 'I'm starving.'

He ignored the hand, but moved next to her for the walk back to the main house. 'We have to talk,' he growled, grabbing her arm above the elbow and steering her down the walk.

After a few silent paces she cast her eyes downward and asked weakly, 'Why does it upset you so much?' knowing she wouldn't have to be more specific than that.

'I told you before. There's no room for personal feelings in our relationship. Not if you want to see again.'

'And how do you stop personal feelings?'

'By not letting them start.'

She smiled then, and raised her head. 'Then we've failed already,' she said happily. 'So let's give up.'

'Cassie,' he said tiredly, drawing out her name. 'Casual sex with female patients just isn't my style. It hurts everybody.'

She heard the tremor in his voice, and her spirits lifted. 'Casual sex?'

She stopped and reached for his arm, pressing through the cloth of his shirt when he tried to pull away. 'I don't think it would be casual,' she whispered, 'and that's why you're so afraid of it. You're afraid to love.'

'Love?' he spat disdainfully. 'And what would you know about love? What did you ever have a chance to learn in that Park Avenue ivory tower about love? Real life isn't a fairy tale, Cassie. People don't fall in love in a week. And physical needs don't always have love to justify them. We desired each other, that's all. There's a difference between that kind of hunger and love.'

His voice was hard, running rampant over the words

with a strident urgency, but there was something else
there; something halting and deep and full of promise,
that was what Cassie heard.

'You're only playing with words,' she persisted,
trotting to keep pace as he pulled away from her with
long, determined strides. 'I'm in love now. With you.'
She chuckled suddenly, and covered her mouth with her
hand, stifling the thrust of amusement that had no place
in a conversation that would determine the course of
her life. 'Good Lord, that's terrible, isn't it?' she said
quickly. 'I've fallen in love with my psychiatrist. How
classic.'

'It's worse than that,' he said sharply. 'It's ridiculous.
It's a childish notion, a little-girl fantasy; and it's simply
not true. You can't possibly take it seriously, and
neither can I. You haven't even talked to any other man
alone—you said that yourself—it's only natural that
you should think you love the first one you get to
know.' He shook his head and exhaled strongly through
his lips. 'I should have expected that,' he muttered in
self-reprimand. 'It was stupid of me not to see it
coming.'

Cassie's steps lengthened with the strength of new
confidence. After all, there had been no contempt in his
voice, at least not against her. And he was not denying
any feeling for her; only her feelings for him. But he
couldn't touch that, couldn't destroy it; not unless she
let him.

She smiled mysteriously, walking towards the
pleasant tinkling of the wind chimes, mounting the
porch steps with practised ease, pausing at the door
only long enough to know he was looking at her. Then
she pushed through the door ahead of him and made
her way to the staircase. 'I'll meet you in the dining
room,' she called over her shoulder, then skipped up the
steps like a child.

Wyatt watched her progress in stony silence, then
walked slowly to the dining-room entrance, finding
every movement an exhausting effort. He stopped at the

doorway, leaning against the frame, unaware of the large form rising from a nearby table and approaching him cautiously.

'Wyatt?' Matt Franklin peered into the younger man's face, a worry line drawing his bushy brows together. 'You look terrible. Are you coming down with something?'

Wyatt blinked slowly as his mind registered the familiar face. 'Matt. What are you doing here?' The presence of other diners in the room penetrated his consciousness slowly, as if he were just waking from a long sleep, and he nodded vaguely to those nearby.

Matt frowned, peering deep into the blue chips of eyes that looked ominously vacant. 'Katy's a thunderstorm in the kitchen preparing your dinner for tonight,' he said absently, his thought concentrated on the drawn face of his friend. 'I promised to lunch here and stay out of the way.'

'Oh, dammit,' Wyatt blurted, the haze suddenly clearing. 'I forgot all about that.'

'Come on.' Matt grabbed his arm and steered him towards the table nearest the entrance. 'Sit with me. I've already eaten, but I can dawdle over my coffee for a while.' His voice was edged with concern as he watched Wyatt sink into the chair and lean heavily against its back. 'What's wrong, Wyatt?'

Wyatt's smile was grim. 'Cassie Winters is wrong. All wrong. What else?'

Matt shook his head until the great mane of his frosty hair stood away from his face. 'You're trying too hard, Wyatt; and pushing too hard, if I know you. I don't think Cassie can handle the kind of pressure you dish out.'

Wyatt laughed bitterly. 'Oh, she can handle it all right, Matt. She's a hell of a lot more resilient than I am.'

Even if Matt hadn't seen Cassie enter the room, he would have known she was there by the sudden tension in Wyatt's body. A smile broke through his frown when his gaze shifted to the lithe, lovely body, almost visibly quivering with the energy of youth. She walked straight to their table with barely a pause and smiled, extending her hand. 'Hello, Dr Franklin, she greeted him.

He rose and closed his big hands around hers, then pulled out a third chair. 'Hello, Cassie. You're even lovelier than I remembered. Soggy, but lovely all the same.'

She laughed as he tucked in her chair. 'We've come directly from the pool. I haven't even had a chance to dry out, I'm afraid.'

'Did you enjoy your swim?' Matt asked carefully, knowing full well what a frightening experience the first blind swim was for all the patients.

'I loved it,' she smiled quietly, 'but it ended much too soon.' Wyatt winced at her words, pulling back into his chair.

'Well.' Matt reclaimed his seat and raised his eyebrows at Wyatt. 'I must say you seem to be adjusting well. By the way, Cassie, how on earth did you know I was here?'

She leaned towards him across the table and her eyes sparkled with mischief. 'I'd like you to think it was some magnificent sixth sense,' she confessed, then added meaningfully, 'but that only works with some people. Actually, I heard you from the hall.'

Matt laughed gently, then turned to Wyatt, concern clouding his features to see the white, strained expression on the younger man's face. 'Katy is expecting you both at six, Wyatt; but I'd recommend an afternoon rest before you come. If you show up at the house looking like that, she's going to strap you in the guest-room bed for the weekend.'

Wyatt shook his head in irritation, but Cassie tensed and asked quickly, 'Looking like what, Dr Franklin? What's wrong with him?'

Matt noted the concern on her face with surprise, then patted her hand reassuringly. 'He just looks tired, Cassie. You've obviously been working him too hard.'

She frowned and narrowed her eyes in Wyatt's direction, as if squinting would enable her to see his face.

'My eyes are bloodshot from the chlorine, that's all,' Wyatt put in quickly, flashing a thunderous glance at Matt, who merely smiled. 'Dr Franklin believes red eyes are a sign of impending illness, and Katy mothers me without mercy.'

'Oh,' Cassie nodded uncertainly.

'Well, I'll leave you two to your lunch,' Matt said as he rose. 'I'll see you both at six, then?'

'I can't tell you how much I'm looking forward to it, Dr Franklin,' Cassie smiled up at him. Sitting down to a family dinner will be a wonderful change.'

Matt patted her head in a paternal gesture, and scowled a fond warning at Wyatt. 'I want both of you fresh tonight. Don't do anything draining this afternoon.'

There was an awkward silence after he left, broken only by Helen's appearance to take their orders. She was as icily reserved as always but, for once, Cassie paid no attention to the woman's ill-concealed hostility toward her.

'Well?' she asked after Helen left. 'Are you?'

'Am I what?'

'Exhausted. You must look ghastly, for Dr Franklin to have made such a fuss.'

'He's just like that,' he answered a little sharply. 'He worries like a doting father. Imagines problems that aren't there.'

'I see,' she said doubtfully, and silence descended once again. 'It's me, isn't it?' she asked finally. 'You're worried about my treatment, aren't you?'

He rubbed rubbed his chin absently with one hand, then decided to be honest. It was the only thing left to try. 'We're running out of time, Cassie. There's only a week left, and yes, I'm worried. I lie awake nights worrying about it.'

She imagined him lying against a white pillow, his eyes wide in the dark, thinking of her.

'I think you're ready,' he continued, 'emotionally and physically, to face whatever memory made you blind, but the way you react to me personally is holding you back.' He sighed and closed his eyes. 'It may be that I shouldn't be treating you at all. This relationship you imagine we have is standing in your way.'

She lowered her eyes and examined the pattern on the silverware with her fingers. 'I'm not imagining a relationship,' she said softly. 'It's real, and you know it as well as I do.'

Her unshakable certainty frustrated him, and he sighed noisily in exasperation.

'It won't go away, Wyatt.'

He was so lost in his own troubled thoughts that he didn't bother to bristle at her use of his first name. 'You're wrong,' he said quietly. 'It will go away, in time.'

He covered one of her hands with his, trying to temper the harshness of what he was about to say. She turned her hand under his, curling slender fingers around the broad expanse of his palm, pressing lightly with her fingertips between the smooth ridges the bones made on the top of his hand. Even this relatively innocent touch was almost unbearably erotic, and he fumbled for the right words.

'Cassie. Your feelings aren't really extraordinary. In fact, they were almost boringly predictable. Patients often think they're falling in love with their doctors. Psychiatrists in particular . . .'

'Don't lecture me on love transference, Wyatt. I've read all about it, and in this case, it just doesn't apply,' she said certainly.

'It's natural that you should feel that way. If you think you're in love, the love seems real.'

She smiled with that ancient, inbred wisdom of women who tolerate the foolish notions of beloved men and children. 'Believe what you like, Wyatt. It won't stop me from being in love with you.'

He leaned forward and spoke urgently. 'That's not possible, Cassie. You must recognise it for the illusion it is, or my treatment will be totally ineffective.'

'And if I pretend you don't attract me, will you also be able to pretend that I don't attract you?' she mocked him.

He was completely silent, and her free hand felt for his face, and found it hot. He jerked his head away from her hand and she withdrew it slowly, letting it fall back to the table.

Wyatt closed his eyes in frustration, trying to block out the vision of her face, and failing miserably. Even with his eyes closed, he could still see her—wet tendrils of hair clinging damply to her neck; eyes wide and guileless; full, sensuous lips parted in a moist circle. His forehead furrowed with the intensity of his concentration, and he felt the first sharp warning of a headache building behind his eyes. 'It isn't real, Cassie,' he repeated slowly. 'You have to realise that.'

He pulled his hand away from hers, and shrugged off her attempts to reach for his shoulder. 'You're making progress, and it's elated you. You become more self-assured every day. You're finding the strength to explore your own past, when you aren't distracted by the present, and because I'm responsible for that progress, you're grateful to me. So subconsciously, you decide to offer your love as payment. It's that simple,' he finished, taking a deep breath.

Cassie merely smiled. 'You make it all sound very dry, and very clinical.'

'And very predictable, which it was. It happens often.'

'All your women patients fall in love with you?' she teased.

'A lot of them do—or think they do.' Then he added quickly, 'But only temporarily. The feeling fades quickly once they recognise it for what it is. His eyes flew wide as her hand crept under the table to rest on his thigh, and he shoved his chair backward with a sudden thrust of his legs.

'And do they all make you this nervous?' she asked, still smiling.

'They're not all as brazen as you, thank God,' he whispered angrily.

She was up from her chair so quickly that he would not have had time to prevent her actions, even if he could have foreseen them. Suddenly she was squarely in his lap with her hands on either side of his face, and he felt his cheeks flush a hot red with embarrassment as he moved his eyes desperately from side to side to check the reactions of the other people in the room. 'Dammit, Cassie!' he hissed, trying at all costs to maintain a shred of dignity by avoiding a scene. 'Get off me! The room is filled with people!'

'I don't see any people,' she murmured against his mouth, flicking with her tongue against the soft tissue inside his upper lip. His body snapped to attention under the sensation, and for an instant, his mouth softened and opened under hers, and she sensed, rather than heard, a moan building in his throat. Then with surprising strength, his hands spanned her waist and lifted her bodily from his lap. She heard a few scattered titters from various points in the room, and slipped back into her chair with a contented smile, acutely aware of the sound of Wyatt trying to control his breathing. She was not aware of Helen's silent, sinister presence on her left, and jumped when she spoke.

'I hope I'm not interrupting,' she said acidly, 'but your lunch is ready.'

She plunked down both plates with uncommon carelessness, spilling wine sauce on the snowy cloth in front of Wyatt. He was too embarrassed to meet her eyes in silent reprimand; too furious to trust himself to speak for many moments after she had gone. When he did, his voice shook with a cold rage.

'Don't ever, ever, try anything like that again!' he

said slowly, drawing each word out into a distinct hiss.
'I will not have you parade your childish fantasies in
front of the staff. Do you understand?'

Cassie sat in wide-eyed silence, stunned by the
itensity of his reaction. She had only kissed him,
after all. What could be so horrible about that? 'No,'
she pouted in genuine confusion, 'I don't understand.'

'And you never will!' he shot back contemptuously.
'And that's the problem. You've been locked up too
long to ever deal with the real world, and I was a fool
not to see it before. I should probably thank you for
making it so crystal clear. The illusion of treating a
woman is completely gone, and I think I'll find treating
a child a great deal easier.'

There was the cold, cruel ring of finality in his voice,
and Cassie trembled to hear it, knowing deeply and
immediately that at this moment, he hated her.

'I've embarrassed you,' she whispered, horrified by
the realisation that something so spontaneous, so clean
and honest, could have such disastrous consequences.
'I'm sorry.'

The indifference of his reply chilled her. 'Finish your
lunch; then you can have the rest of the afternoon to
yourself. I'd like to avoid dinner with the Franklins, but
that would require an explanation I'm not prepared to
make, so we'll just have to muddle through it. I'll pick
you up at 5:45.'

Her hands fell uselessly to her lap, and her gaze was
steady and unblinking. 'I'm not hungry,' she said softly,
pushing away from the table.

'Suit yourself,' he replied coldly, and watched her rise
and walk stiffly from the room.

She sagged against the wall on the other side of the
dining-room door, wondering miserably if his anger
would fade, and if it did, if there would be anything left
beneath it. Her feet dragged like leaden weights as she
stumbled across the foyer and pulled herself up the stairs.

In the dining room behind her, Wyatt passed a hand

across his mouth angrily, then the fingers hesitated at the point that her tongue had touched, and his hand quivered, remembering the sensation.

CHAPTER TEN

CASSIE hunched in the bucket seat of Wyatt's small sports car, feeling as awkward and as uncomfortable as she had ever felt in her life.

Pot holes in the old, winding road they were travelling shot through the car's stiff suspension in painful little jolts that only added to her discomfort.

Wyatt had said nothing but the mandatory greeting when he picked her up at the main house, and had remained stonily silent since. She still stung from his rebuke at lunch, and his obvious indifference to her presence was shredding any conviction she might have had that her strong feelings for him were reciprocal. His flat rejection had shattered her resolve, and she curled inward in defensive apathy.

Wyatt tried to keep his eyes firmly fastened on the road, but occasionally, under the pretence of glancing out of the passenger window, his gaze brushed over the huddled, silent form on his right. He negotiated a narrow, twisting drive through towering white pines, and brought the car to a gentle stop before the graceful colonial building, oddly out of place on the heavily wooded lot.

'We're here,' he said quietly, pulling on the parking brake and turning his head to look fully at Cassie for the first time.

'I don't think I mentioned that you look very nice tonight. That's a lovely dress.' He blinked hard at his own understatement, allowing his eyes to linger for just a moment longer.

The dress was a vibrant moss green silk, a luxuriously rich background for the pale mass of hair she had brushed over her shoulders. Instead of diffusing the blue depths of her eyes, the dress's colour somehow made them seem more startling and intense. He caught his gaze dropping to the point where the v-neck joined just above the swell of her breasts, and hastily opened his door.

When he took her hand to help her up from the low seat, she grasped his fingers tightly and stood firmly in the way so he couldn't close the car door. 'Wyatt,' she said hesitantly, and then laughed softly. 'Dr Field. I have to say this, or the evening will be unbearable.' She lifted her hand to touch his cheek lightly, and let her palm remain pressed against his jaw, smooth with recent shaving, her thumb resting against the corner of his mouth. 'I want to apologise for what happened at lunch. If nothing else, it was inconsiderate of me to expose you to that kind of embarrassment in front of the people you work with.'

He looked deeply into the unseeing eyes, and reached up to cover her hand with his without thinking. Pressing it even more firmly against his cheek was an unconscious gesture, and he didn't realise he had done it.

'Can you forgive me for that?' she asked plaintively, and he tightened his grip on her hand, pulling it over to where he could press his lips into her palm.

A lock of his hair fell across her fingers as he bent his head, and her pulse quickened uncontrollably. She pulled her hand away immediately, shaken by her own helpless reaction, confused by his gentle response.

'I'm the one who should apologise, Cassie,' he murmured. 'I was more angry with myself than with you, and I was too harsh. I've handled this whole thing badly. Can we go on as friends? Or at least under a flag of truce? We can continue with your treatment from here, forget today entirely.'

She nodded with a sad smile, wondering how she would ever manage to forget this day, or manage to pretend she felt nothing of consequence for the man before her. It was almost too much to ask, when the recollection of his body straining against hers in the pool was still so vivid.

'Well, come on in, you two!' Dr Franklin called from the doorway of the house. 'We can't hold your reservations forever!'

Katy Franklin shook her head in smiling appreciation when she was introduced to Cassie a few moments later. 'My word, child!' she exclaimed. 'Do you have any idea of how beautiful you are? And has Matthew asked you to run away with him yet?'

Cassie blushed at the compliment and the tease, and lowered her head with a bashful smile.

Not one to ever countenance shyness, Katy grabbed both her hands and led her over to a long couch in the living room adjacent to the foyer, and pulled her down next to her.

'It's so nice of you to have me for dinner, Mrs Franklin,' Cassie said quietly.

'Nonsense,' Katy punctuated her impatience with a pat on Cassie's hand. 'And call me Katy, for Heaven's sake. I couldn't manage an entire evening being called Mrs Franklin. The pressure would be too much. I'd have to be on my best behaviour to deserve such a title, and as Matt and Wyatt will tell you, there's no such thing.'

'I'll vouch for that,' Wyatt's voice came from the foyer. 'You've already ignored one of your guests completely. You have no manners at all, Katy.'

Cassie frowned at the tone of Wyatt's voice. It held a warmth and a playful tenderness she had never heard before.

'Excuse me, dear,' Katy whispered in her ear. 'I have to go embrace that extremely good-looking man who followed you here, or I'll never hear the end of it.'

Wyatt smiled with genuine fondness at the short woman who approached him with open arms, still managing to look elegantly graceful in spite of her stature and her body's frustrating tendency towards plumpness. She hugged him warmly and planted a noisy kiss on his cheek. 'Hello, dear. You look a little tired. Are you feeling all right?'

'Stop it, Katy,' he laughed, pushing her away by the

shoulders and holding her gently in front of him. 'Matt has already cast aspersions on my good looks once today. My ego couldn't handle another slice. Especially not from the most beautiful woman alive.'

Katy patted the short cap of her salt-and-pepper hair with affected modesty, then laughed. 'I'm gracefully passing on that title to Cassie,' she said, looking over towards the couch. 'I'm afraid there's absolutely no contest. Now come and sit down, no, over there, in the easy chair. Matthew has been playing at the bar again, whipping up some dreadful concoction they served at his last convention, and we're all to be guinea pigs.'

'I heard that,' Dr Franklin scolded as he served the drinks, and Cassie envied the recipient of the deep affection in his voice. 'And you're going to eat your words, or rather, drink them. This is without question one of the finest cocktails you'll ever be served.'

'And the most colourful,' Katy said, eyeing the bright red mixture in her glass sceptically.

'It's marvellous.' Cassie sipped from her glass and ran her tongue over her upper lip with a smile.

'Now there's a girl with taste,' Dr Franklin beamed. 'Cassie's a city girl, Katy. Did I tell you that?'

'You certainly did not,' Katy said petulantly, sinking into the couch next to Cassie. 'And I went ahead and prepared a down-home country meal. You'll have to rough it, Cassie. The food we're having tonight is probably a bit different than what you're used to. I'm a simple cook, I'm afraid.'

'Whatever it is, it smells wonderful. Like . . .' Cassie closed her eyes and a tiny line appeared between her brows.

Wyatt's eyes narrowed as he watched her face. 'Like what, Cassie?' he prompted.

'Like our kitchen used to smell on the cook's night off, when my mother would cook,' she mused.

Wyatt shot a glance at Matt and nodded, while Katy watched the silent eye signals in puzzlement. All Matthew had told her was that the young patient coming to dinner was suffering a form of selective amnesia, and that Wyatt hoped a home environment would stir up old memories. So far, at least, they seemed to be succeeding.

But there was something else Matthew hadn't mentioned. Something so obvious that one would have to be a fool not to see it—or blind, she thought with a smile. And her husband was neither. She leaned back on the couch and unconsciously took Cassie's hand, watching the faces of her husband and her guests as they made idle conversation, reading shrewdly between every line.

'Are you going to the seminar next month, Wyatt?' Matt was asking.

Katy drained the last of her drink and rose from the couch. 'That does it,' she said perfunctorily. 'If they're going to talk shop, Cassie, we might as well get out of here. We'll make dinner, they can do the dishes.'

'You want me to help?' Cassie asked incredulously, looking up at where Katy stood, with an expression of delighted disbelief. It was not the response Katy had expected, and her heart went out to the young woman who thought being asked to help in the kitchen was an honour.

Katy took her hand and helped her up from the couch. 'I can't stand being in the kitchen alone,' she explained with a laugh, 'and from the looks of those two, I wouldn't be able to pry either one out of their chairs. Do you mind?'

'Oh, no,' Cassie said quickly. 'If you're sure I won't be in the way.'

'Not a chance. You're going to be too busy. Matt, if you'll refill our glasses with some more of that ghastly red stuff, I'll come back for them in a minute. Come on, dear. The kitchen is this way.'

Cassie followed her eagerly through a swinging door that opened on to a room that felt bright and airy.

'Why don't you sit here at the table?' Katy directed. 'I'll bring you the relishes and a tray to fill.'

Cassie inhaled deeply of the odours around her forgetting to be nervous about facing a task totally unfamiliar. She heard the thunks of half a dozen different containers being set on the table before her and separated the smells of olives, various kinds of pickles, carrots and celery.

'Here's the dish, Cassie. Arrange it however you like I'm going after our drinks.'

'Katy,' Matt questioned her quietly when she returned to the living room. 'What's come over you You've never dragged a guest into the kitchen before much less asked that they help prepare their own meal.'

She pressed her full lips together impatiently as she accepted the two glasses. 'You told me you wanted to duplicate a family atmosphere, remember?' she whispered. 'Well, what could be more motherly than having a daughter help in the kitchen? Now stop fussing.'

Matt smiled and shrugged as he watched his wife bustle back through the swinging door.

Cassie raised her head with an expectant smile at Katy's entrance. 'How am I doing?' she asked with a tentative pride that touched Katy with its poignancy.

'It's beautiful, dear,' she said gently, 'but you're much too fast. Would you mind seasoning the potato salad? I'm running behind.'

'Potato salad?' Cassie asked uncertainly, her smile fading.

Katy brought an enormous crockery bowl over to the table. 'Like I said, this is a country meal. Almost a picnic, actually. Fried chicken, potato salad, vegetables from the garden, and apple pie. Here. Salt and pepper at two o'clock, paprika at three.'

Dismay crossed Cassie's face, and she hesitated. 'I feel so useless,' she said sadly, 'but I don't know how to season potato salad, or anything else, for that matter. I've never cooked in my life.'

'No problem,' Katy replied breezily. 'Just taste it, and add seasoning until you think it's right. Go on. Be daring. Potato salad is kind to new cooks. It's almost impossible to ruin it.'

'All right,' Cassie said hesitantly, and furrowed her brows in concentration as she plunged a large wooden spoon into the huge bowl.

Katy smiled at the earnest expression on the lovely face while she busied herself at the stove. 'This is nice,' she said absently. 'Reminds me of teaching Marianne—she's my daughter—how to cook. We spent a lot of time together in this room.'

'Dr Field told me she had married and moved away. You must miss her.'

'Very much. That's why having you here is such a treat for me.'

Cassie frowned as she shook the salt shaker over the bowl tentatively. 'I would think you'd get tired of having patients from Windrow visit.'

'Hardly!' Katy laughed. 'You're my very first. I've never even met one of the Windrow students before, let alone fed one, in all the years we've been here.'

'Really?' Cassie lifted her head in amazement. 'Then why . . .?'

Katy pursed her lips and wiped her hands on her apron. She never was any good at deception. 'Frankly, I wondered why myself,' she admitted, taking a seat next to Cassie at the table. 'Here's your drink. The beans need another ten minutes at least, so we'll take a break.' She took a long sip from her glass and hoped whatever Matthew had put into it wasn't too intoxicating. 'Matthew told me only that you had an unusual type of amnesia, and that Wyatt hoped a home environment might jog your memory, and help you regain your sight.'

Cassie nodded sadly. 'My mother was killed in the same car accident that blinded me,' she said simply. 'I can't remember anything about it.'

Katy's features sagged in sympathy, and she sighed deeply. 'I see,' she said. 'Then I suppose it makes sense. I must represent the mother figure in this little plan. That's why you're here. One reason, anyway.'

Cassie sighed, disappointed and almost embarrassed to learn the evening was simply a clinical experiment, and that this wonderful woman was being used as a part of it.

'But I think Matt had an ulterior motive,' Katy continued quickly, squeezing Cassie's hand. 'Aside from the fact that he took a shine to you himself, and knew I would love having you here, I think he was testing a secret suspicion of his own.'

'What suspicion?'

Katy hesitated for a moment, and then smiled. 'That you and Wyatt are in love, of course.'

'What?' Cassie asked weakly.

'Oh, my dear, it's so obvious that it's almost comical. Especially since you both go to such lengths to pretend it isn't so—even to each other! I don't think I've ever seen two people try so hard not to be in love.'

Cassie sat absolutely still, her lips parted in amazement.

'Don't look so surprised, child,' Katy patted her cheek affectionately. 'If you could only see the way Wyatt looks at you, especially when he doesn't think anyone else is paying attention, you'd understand how obvious it really is. And you're not much better at trying to hide it, you know. What I don't understand is why on earth either of you try to fight it at all. Love isn't all that bad.'

Cassie's eyes were brimming as she reached with both hands for Katy's face, feeling a sudden, desperate need to know what this woman looked like. Katy sat quietly under the inspection of fluttering fingers, wondering at the expression on Cassie's face.

'What is it, dear?' she asked gently, watching the first tear spill from the sightless eyes, feeling inexplicably close to crying herself. And then she pulled Cassie instinctively into a warm, comforting embrace, feeling a sharp reminder of how it once felt to comfort her own daughter. Cassie returned the hug shyly, then completely, and mourned again a mother

who had been dead for eighteen years. And then she
began to talk.

Katy listened patiently as Cassie stumbled through
the frustrations of the past week, blushing silently at the
intimate moments, realising that Cassie was too
innocent to understand that such things were usually
kept private, not relayed to a relative stranger over a
bowl of potato salad on a late summer evening. But
then she didn't feel like a stranger; and Cassie didn't
think of her as one.

In the silence that followed the telling, they could
both hear the murmurs of soft conversation from the
other room, and the slow, chaotic bubbling of beans left
too long on the stove.

Cassie realised she had been babbling, but there was
no embarrassment at all. Katy's arms were warm and
relaxed around her, still around her after all that time;
and it felt so good to be held quietly, sheltered
somehow, safe in the comforting embrace of another
human being.

It wasn't like the quick, fierce hugs of Mrs Carmody,
who could never unbend quite enough to make a
motherless child feel affection, no matter how hard she
tried, or how much she loved. This was unconditional
cherishing from a woman who gave unconditionally,
and for the first time since her mother had died, Cassie
felt the warmth of spontaneous affection, and wondered
if perhaps she might not deserve it.

'It was much too easy, Cassie,' Katy was saying
gently, 'for Wyatt to convince you he felt nothing, when
all the signs were there, just screaming the truth. Do
you think so little of yourself, that it was easier to
believe he didn't care than he did?'

Cassie moved reluctantly from the older woman's
embrace and wiped her eyes. 'He was very convincing,'
she said artlessly. 'And he still is.'

'And will probably continue to be,' Katy smiled.
'Loving is a brand new experience for Wyatt, you
know. He's always been afraid to give; afraid to get

involved. Besides that, he's your doctor. They're not allowed to fall in love with patients, remember. That's strictly forbidden.'

Cassie shook her head sceptically. 'I hope that's all it is. I keep thinking there must be something else. Something deeper.'

Katy touched Cassie's cheek lightly with one hand. 'He loves you,' she said simply. 'It's as plain as the nose on your face.'

'I can't see my nose, Katy,' Cassie reminded her with a wry smile.

'But that doesn't mean it isn't there, now does it?'

Cassie was quietly radiant as they all took their seats at the dining room table, and even Wyatt sensed the silent air of conspiracy between the two women.

He had no way of knowing what had occurred behind the closed kitchen door, and felt vaguely uneasy, as if he had lost control once again. He remembered feeling precisely the same way when Cassie had emerged from the locker room only that morning, and realised that whatever had passed between Katy and Cassie had restored the contentment he had so effectively shattered at lunch. Once again she seemed strangely satisfied and self-confident, and he regretted the impulse that had prompted him to bring her here. There was no defence against Cassie's mind when she was happy; no way to penetrate the black wall of her blindness as long as she was content with it.

He gazed at the serenity of her face with sadness, knowing he would have to destroy that serenity at the first opportunity.

He sighed deeply and scolded Katy with a dark, silent scowl she didn't understand, resigning himself to an evening of quiet endurance. He could do nothing here, in front of Matt and Katy. Tomorrow, perhaps, when he had Cassie alone, away from the silent, moral support of his friends. Then he would begin again.

* * *

Matt closed the door softly after Cassie and Wyatt left hours later, and turned to smile sheepishly at his wife. 'You enjoyed having them, didn't you?' he asked in a futile attempt to make idle conversation.

Katy forced herself to frown with disapproval and put both hands on her hips. 'Why didn't you tell me?' she demanded. 'And you might as well wipe that innocent look off your face. It doesn't fool me after all these years. You knew those kids were in love.'

Matt shrugged and pulled the warm, soft comfort of his wife's body into his arms. 'I thought Wyatt might be,' he smiled. 'But I needed confirmation from an expert. If I'd said anything ahead of time, I might have influenced your judgment.'

'Well, I hope you talked to Wyatt,' she grumbled. 'He's trying to convince Cassie that her feelings are love transference, or some such nonsense, and that he has no feelings for her at all. It's breaking the poor girl's heart, and she has enough problems without having to deal with that.'

Matt smiled and pulled her closer. 'You liked her, didn't you?'

'More than that,' she sighed, reaching for the light switch and pulling him towards the bedroom. 'And she's just right for Wyatt. It's high time he was married.'

'Katy!' Matt laughed. 'Aren't you pushing things a little?'

'People who love each other should get married,' she said decisively, planting a kiss squarely on his mouth. 'Besides, if Wyatt marries Cassie, they'll live here, and that fits in with my plans perfectly. I promised to teach her how to cook.'

Matt smiled in tender exasperation, and Katy frowned up to him, suddenly serious. 'Will you talk to him, Matt? He is making a mistake, you know.'

'I don't know, Katy. Love transference isn't always such nonsense. It happens often. I'm not certain that Wyatt's fears in that direction aren't justified. Besides, I can't interfere in his private life like that. He'd never forgive me.'

'Oh, you doctors!' she muttered under her breath. 'Nothing is simple for you, even the obvious! Now are you going to talk to him, or shall I?'

From past experience, Matt knew that it was easier to agree with his wife once she had made up her mind, than it was to try to change it. 'All right, Katy,' he sighed in surrender. 'I'll go against my better judgment and try to broach the subject, but only to save him from one of your browbeatings. And if he never speaks to us again, it's on your head.'

She nodded with satisfaction. 'Tomorrow.'

'Tomorrow! Tomorrow's Saturday!'

'I know that.'

'But it's my day off. I wasn't even going to Windrow tomorrow!'

'It won't take long, Matthew. You'll be home by noon,' she smiled sweetly, then turned down the covers on the bed.

CHAPTER ELEVEN

CASSIE wakened the next morning feeling a deep, solid contentment that was a brand new entry in her catalogue of emotions. Her blindness, her uncertain future, the death of her father—all faded pleasantly into a murky mist that seemed unrelated to the here and now. Katy had confirmed that Wyatt loved her, and everything else was incidental by comparison.

She smiled, remembering the evening before. The warm, companionable atmosphere she and Wyatt had shared at the Franklins carried over through the short ride home, and Cassie had been content to bask in the presence of a Wyatt Field she had never met before. Temporarily freed from the grinding pressures of his role as her psychiatrist, he had been quick to laugh; thoughtful, and a warm conversationalist. She had not questioned the sudden change in his attitude towards her, knowing intuitively that the presence of the Franklins somehow protected her from Wyatt Field, the psychiatrist, and introduced her for the first time to Wyatt Field, the man. And Wyatt Field, the man, loved her. Even Katy had seen that.

The urgency of physical contact had mellowed with the confident realisation that they had all their lives before them, and her parting from him had been unstrained with the need to confirm their relationship. She had been content to leave him with a simple good night, certain for the first time that there were hundreds of good nights yet to come.

And now there would be no more hedging, no more pretence. With the gift of Katy's sight, she had seen the only thing she needed to know.

Wyatt was waiting at the bottom of the stairs when she came down. 'We're going to have breakfast on the porch this morning,' he announced. 'There's a storm brewing west of here, and this may be our last shot at fresh air for the day.'

She agreed willingly, and preceded him out the front door. At his direction, she followed the porch railing to the western corner, found the wrought iron back of a chair with her hands, and took her seat. A waiter brought coffee and a fragrant basket of sweet rolls while she examined the heavy matt tablecloth and the dishes before her with her fingers.

'Continental this morning?' she asked, noting the absence of a full setting.

'That's right. They serve brunch on weekends, so a light breakfast is mandatory. Of course, if you'd like something more substantial, all you need do is ask.' His voice seemed a little stilted, and she could tell that his face was turned away from her.

'No, this is fine. I'm still full from last night.'

She took a deep breath and smiled, remembering, for some reason, her first dive off the high board as a child. And then she turned her face towards him and said it, right out; no hesitation, no preliminaries, no uncertainty.

'I know you love me, Wyatt.' The words were soft, quick, and breathless.

There was a long silence, then she heard his cup settling quietly in his saucer.

Wyatt turned his head away and looked out over the lawn. White-topped thunderheads loomed over the horizon, like an enormous quilt being pulled over the blue sky. The storm would be bad, when it broke. 'I thought we had this settled, Cassie. Once and for all.' He refused to look at her.

'Even Katy could see it,' she persisted gently. 'I almost believed you. I almost believed that there was nothing there, that I had been wrong; but Katy saw it, and she told me. Why do you keep denying it? Pretending it isn't there? Is it because I'm your patient? Is that the only reason?'

The thunderheads rolled steadily eastward, picking up speed, and now Wyatt could just begin to see the slow boil as one weather front met another far in the distance. He shifted in his chair, then dropped his eyelids in silent resignation.

'My mother was blind,' he said absently, staring into the distance.

Now why was he telling her this, Cassie wondered. Whatever did that have to do with anything?

'From a fall from a horse, no less,' he continued. 'A very classy way to be blinded in her social circles. They brought her in from the fields while the rest of the party went on with the hunt. Isn't that incredible? As if she were a casualty of war, and the troops had to go on without her.' He paused to sip from his cup, his eyes still on the horizon. 'She was an active woman; very physical. She couldn't deal with infirmity in anyone, least of all herself. She lingered for a while, or I guess languished would be a better word, then she killed herself.'

Cassie sat absolutely still, breathing through her mouth, afraid to interrupt the quiet, musing soliloquy with even an expression of sympathy.

'You asked me once what made me so intolerant of the blind, Cassie,' he said lifelessly, 'and that's what did it, I suppose. Watching my mother turn inside herself, ignoring the things in her life that should have been more important than sight. I hated her for that, and when she died, I hated her for deserting me. A child's vengeance,' he chuckled coldly. 'Later I learned to hate the weakness that made her do it. It's what I fight against with my patients; what I've always fought against.'

He rubbed a hand across his forehead and his fingers came away damp. The breeze had stopped, and the air was heavy and still.

He turned his head slowly to look at her, his dark hair blending with the blackening clouds behind him, his eyes pinpoints of light against the shadows crossing his face. When he spoke again, his voice was flat and toneless.

'I'm fond of you, Cassie, as I'm fond of most of my patients. And because I'm human, I'm attracted to you physically. But love? Even you should be able to understand now why I could never love you. You're a living example of the kind of weakness that made my mother kill herself, and I hate it.' His voice lowered to a dull whisper. 'But I think you're even worse than she was. She, at least, had no choice about her blindness. You're blind because you want to be. Now you tell me, what's to love about that?'

She blinked slowly several times, wondering absently why she didn't feel anything. His words had seemed to drain her body of all substance, and now she felt empty, almost lighter than air. Light enough to separate from the fragile shell sitting at the table; to hang suspended above the body of the woman she had been just moments before. I'm not part of it, she thought calmly. I'm not really here, in this body, so it can't hurt me. For one painful instant she allowed her defences to fall away, and then she wondered how Katy could have been so wrong. But it didn't really matter anymore. A quirk of fate, a cruel twist of circumstance, made her remind Wyatt of an ugly part of his past, and that barrier was too strong to tear down. Whatever they might have felt for each other could never overcome that, and she understood at last that he was beyond her reach, and there wasn't a thing she could do about it.

Although she felt only numbness, her face was serene with acceptance, and Wyatt's expression softened with regret as he looked at her. 'Matt wants to see me for a few minutes in the medical building,' he said quietly. His voice held a peculiar touch of sadness, but Cassie didn't hear it. The senses that had strained for so many days to hear the emotion behind the words, now heard only the words themselves.

She forced a small smile and nodded, and heard herself say, 'I see. That's fine.'

'I shouldn't be long. When I get back, we'll talk.'

'All right, Dr Field.'

She lifted her cup to her lips and swallowed automatically, but never felt the lukewarm coffee slide down her throat. Some remote part of her mind recorded the fact that he had left the table and descended the porch steps, and was now crossing the common. The morning air was so still that she could hear the hiss of the door close as he entered the medical building yards away, even over the distant splash of water in the fountain.

She rose from the table purposefully, but without hurry, and obeyed a command that came from deep within her brain to leave the house, and to walk. Her stride was long and steady as she circled to the back of the house and moved surely through the strip of brush towards the woods. She looked straight ahead, her chin lifted, her eyes placid and unseeing, and she thought of nothing.

Behind her, dark clouds blackened a full half of the blue sky, and leaves just beginning to colour trembled in the first whisper of the wind to come.

By the time Cassie had crossed the strip of brush behind the main house, Wyatt was already dismissing Matt Franklin's discomfort at invading his friend's privacy. 'It doesn't matter, Matt. If it's that obvious, you have every right to question me about my relationship with Cassie. Besides, I know you only brought it up because you . . . care.'

'More than you know,' Matt said with quiet sincerity. 'But I still wouldn't have mentioned it if I hadn't been coerced. You know that. Katy threatened to talk to you herself if I didn't. I thought I'd spare you that, at least.'

Wyatt's smile was grim. 'I never could fool Katy, could I? Or you either, for that matter.'

Matt leaned forward on his elbows. 'But you're trying to fool Cassie, Wyatt. Why? Why keep pretending . . .?'

'That I'm not in love with her?' Wyatt shook his head

in self-derision. 'Ridiculous, isn't it? Psychiatrist falls in love with patient.'

'But she loves you too, Wyatt. Surely you can see that.'

'Maybe. And if she does, that only makes it worse. You, Matt, of all people, should be able to understand.' He tensed in his chair and his eyes narrowed under an urgent frown. 'You know as well as I do what contentment could do to Cassie now. She'd become complacent. She wouldn't try to change anything. She'd stop trying to remember.' He rubbed at the line between his brows. 'That's what loving Cassie would do—leave her blind. If she's happy without it, she doesn't need her sight. But if sight's the only thing she has left, maybe she'll work for it.'

Matt toyed with a pencil on his desk, watching the pink tip of the eraser bob against the glistening wood. 'Then again,' he said softly, watching Wyatt's expression, 'if you convince her that she's lost you, she may withdraw completely. Give up altogether. It's a terrible risk, Wyatt. You know that, don't you?'

Wyatt's lips curled in a tight, hard smile. 'I know that,' he said flatly. 'But I had to take the chance. I had to convince her I felt nothing. Maybe a new pain will bring back the old pain.'

Matt looked up sharply. 'You *had* to? You've done it already?'

He nodded shortly. 'Moments ago, in fact.' He rose from his chair and wavered slightly. 'And now I'll go back and twist the knife, if I can stand it. I have a chance to force her memory, while she's still vulnerable.'

Matt shook his head sadly, sympathising with the agony of both young people. 'And if it doesn't work, what then?'

Wyatt shrugged slightly, and let the frustration show on his face.

Matt measured the depth of the pain in his young friend's eyes, then gave him a small nod of encouragement. 'Come on,' he said, rising from his chair. 'I'll walk you back to the house.'

The wind caught the side door when Wyatt pushed it open, and flung it against the brick of the outside wall.

'It's going to be a bad one,' Matt commented, hunching his shoulders against the sudden drop in temperature. 'Maybe I'd better head straight home.'

He hesitated before turning for the parking lot and caught Wyatt staring intently across the common towards the main house. 'What is it, Wyatt?'

'She's not there. I left her on the porch, and she's not there.'

Matt glanced over and saw the end of a tablecloth lift and flap in the wind, and heard a faint tinkle as a piece of glassware tumbled. 'She's no fool, Wyatt. The temperature must have dropped twenty degrees since I got here this morning. She probably went back inside.'

Wyatt nodded absently, his eyes still on the porch, his mind troubled by a vague sense of foreboding. He started for the house at a fast walk, not even bothering to turn to Matt before he left.

'Call me!' Matt cried after him, but his words were snatched away by a sudden, violent gust of wind.

She wasn't in the house. Not in any of the downstairs rooms, or in her own, either. The elusive dread that had only tapped him on the shoulder before became an icy fist around his heart as Wyatt raced through the house, flinging open doors. He burst into the kitchen and shouted questions at the help, who merely shook their heads, startled by the appearance of a breathless, wild-eyed man in their midst who bore little resemblance to the staid, aloof Dr Field they knew.

He emerged in a rush back on to the front porch and stopped dead for a moment, listening to his heart pound in his ears. The tablecloth flapped madly in the wind now, stained where fallen cups and glasses had spilled their contents in long, narrow streaks that looked like pointed fingers.

Wyatt's eyes jerked quickly to the threatening sky, then he ran back into the house and pulled the receiver off the foyer phone with a clammy hand.

CHAPTER TWELVE

CASSIE'S toe caught on an exposed root and she tumbled forward, catching herself at the last moment with outstretched palms that smacked hard into the dry soil. She pushed herself up and brushed her hands thoughtlessly on her jeans, then plodded forward without further hesitation.

There was a faint, tingling warning in the back of her mind; a suspicion that she should have crested the hill by now, that the incline she was travelling was steeper than the one she and Wyatt had climbed the other day, but it didn't seem to matter. Being lost was unimportant. She was on her way to somewhere, and the physical effort was soothing in itself.

She didn't notice the ominous whistle of wind high above in the delicate tracery of late growth topping ancient trees. She didn't notice the seeping chill of air growing steadily colder. If anything, she felt too warm.

Droplets of perspiration pulled the thin fabric of her blouse against her back, and her body temperature rose slightly as blood rushed to fulfil the demands of exertion. She kept climbing as Matt and Wyatt talked in the medical building; climbing as they emerged from the side door on to the common; climbing as Wyatt raced through the main house in panic. Eventually she topped a ragged, primitive ridge a full mile from Windrow's cultured lawns, just as Wyatt's hand reached for the phone.

She sagged against the gnarled trunk of a scrub oak to catch her breath, and a gust of wind flattened her damp blouse against her spine. It felt like a clammy hand pressed firmly against her, and for the first time, she heard the wind and the distant rumble of thunder, and suddenly she was cold.

*   *   *

Maggie burst through the front door with a gust of howling wind that swept through the foyer and lifted the fronds of the ferns down the hall. The area was filled with staff members milling about in aimless urgency, waiting for direction. Wyatt broke through a cluster of people and started for the door, and Maggie knew the moment she saw his face that Cassie had not been found.

'Good Lord, Wyatt! What happened to you?' she asked as she rushed up to him, taking in the torn, soiled white shirt, the faint scratches across one cheek where a branch had whipped against his face.

'I was up on the hill. I took her there the other day. I thought she may have gone back.' He paused for a deep breath. 'We've covered the grounds, and all the buildings, Maggie. There's no sign of her.' His voice broke uncharacteristically and he closed his eyes until he had regained control. 'And the police are on their way.'

Maggie reached up gently to brush a black curl from his forehead, her face reflecting sympathy and concern at the same time. 'What can I do, Wyatt?' she asked quickly, and he thanked her with a brief, tight smile for not asking why Cassie had run.

'Organise the mob, Maggie. I've got to get back out there. She's in the woods, somewhere. It's the only place she could be, and we've got to find her. It would be bad enough for a sighted person to be lost in there, but for a blind girl? She doesn't have a chance to find her way back. Especially not in a storm.'

He rushed for the door and Maggie raced after him. 'Here, Wyatt,' she commanded, stripping the poncho slicker over her head. 'This won't cover all of you, but it will help. Put it on.'

'I don't have time, Maggie,' he said impatiently as he reached for the doorknob.

'Then make time!' she said, grabbing his arm. 'The rain will hit soon, and if you find her, she'll need it.'

He dropped his hand from the door and his shoulders

sagged. '*When* I find her,' he corrected.

'Right.'

He pulled the poncho over his head and grabbed Maggie's shoulders. 'Listen, Maggie,' he hissed urgently. 'This isn't the worst of the storm. The cops said the brunt of it won't hit for another hour, and it's bad. It's flattened buildings and downed power lines in Carver County, and it's going to tumble these woods like matchsticks. We *have* to find her before it hits. Have them cover the areas close enough to the house to get back in time. I don't want anybody hurt.'

'I'll take care of it,' she said, pushing him gently on the back. 'Hurry. And make sure you're back in time yourself.'

He flashed a grim smile and disappeared out the door.

When it isn't distorted by senseless panic, the blind person's sense of direction is remarkably accurate. Responding intuitively to sensory input a sighted person might never even acknowledge, the blind can often sense, before others might see, the way out of a maze. So it was that Cassie's subconscious noted and responded to wind, shadow, and terrain, and her trancelike movements eventually returned her unerringly to the edge of the woods near Windrow's main house. But as the trees thinned, her protection from the ever-increasing wind diminished, and for the first time since she left the little table on the porch, an awareness of external conditions began to chip away at the shield her mind's defences had created.

Suddenly, less than a hundred yards from the house, the shield cracked completely, and panic seeped in to claim her mind and dull her senses. She felt the wind tear at her hair, whipping it mercilessly around her face until it felt like she was being slapped awake by hundreds of thin, angry fingers. It penetrated her flimsy blouse with bone-chilling persistence, and pushed against her chest like a giant hand. She shivered convulsively and felt her knees buckle with an exhaustion they had felt long before, and only now admitted. The noise was deafening as the wind buffeted her ears, gusting against branches that scraped each other raw in a mad dance of stiff resistance.

Cassie's head turned desperately from side to side as she tried to command senses now garbled by fear, and her eyes widened in an instinctive, futile attempt to see. She could feel the storm building in a wild crescendo, and backed away from the wind in a thoughtless attempt to escape its wrath. Had she been capable of clear reason at that point, she would have realised that the very protection she sought by backing deeper into the shelter of the trees was taking her farther and farther from the salvation of the Windrow grounds. But reason was beyond her as she succumbed to a deep-seated, instinctive fear of nature's violent moods, and she was reduced to the simple, physical responses of an animal seeking shelter from a storm.

Silent up until now, except for the quick gasps of breath, she felt a scream build within her throat. 'It's just a thunderstorm, Cassie,' she said aloud, and calmed immediately to hear the sound of a human voice, even though it was her own. 'Just a little rain, a little thunder and lightning, that's all.'

She turned and moved a few yards deeper into the shelter of the large trees she sensed closing in around her. 'The wind isn't so bad in here. You can just stay here until the worst is over. Sit it out, rest yourself, and then later, you'll find your way out, or they'll come to find you. There's nothing to worry about. Not really.'

But the wind tore the words from her mouth and whipped them away before she could even hear the comfort of their sound. Her hands found the massive trunk of a sturdy, aged cottonwood, and she felt her way around to the side away from the wind, and sagged to a sitting position against it. The force of the first, fat raindrops broke against the branches above her, and fell more gently to the forest floor where she huddled, shivering with the damp and the cold, jumping to each roll of thunder as the storm bore down.

'Wyatt,' she whispered, hugging her knees and rocking back and forth against the trunk. 'Wyatt, Wyatt, Wyatt.'

The fork of lightning shot from the underbelly of a black mass overhead, streaked down through the crumbling insides of a dying elm a hundred feet from where Cassie cringed, and hit the ground in a violent explosion of sound. She never even heard her own scream.

Then the full force of the wind hit just as the sky opened, and suddenly trees began to creak and bend; dead branches gave up their tenuous holds on living trunks, and the world was filled with the savage sounds of nature pruning a forest. The ground vibrated with the heavy crashes of shallow-rooted pines hitting the forest floor, and eventually Cassie's throat ached from screaming, and the only sound she contributed to the chaos of noise around her was an occasional whimper.

Wyatt dragged himself in through the main door, sodden and dripping, bent with exhaustion and defeat. Maggie rushed to close the door behind him, then quickly moved to help him out of the rain-soaked poncho. She raised her eyebrows at him, but he merely shook his head, his breathing still too laboured for speech.

'Everyone's in the basement,' she said, taking his arm. 'We were afraid you wouldn't make it back, Wyatt. The winds are already over eighty miles an hour.'

'She isn't here then?' he asked weakly. 'You didn't find her?'

Maggie looked once at the ravaged face, then turned quickly away as her eyes began to fill. 'No,' she said in a whisper, and her voice cracked. 'Wyatt! You can't go back out there!' she screamed as he spun away and ran for the door, but her words fell on an empty space where he had been, and the door banged wildly against the frame of the house where he had flung it open.

CHAPTER THIRTEEN

THE storm's fury raged unabated until well past noon, then the world slowly quieted as it moved on, pulling a tracery of angry, wispy grey clouds behind it.

With the danger past, the staff organised quickly to search the graveyard of fallen trees in the woods behind Windrow, but even with every sighted person's aid enlisted, the day grew old without a sign of either Cassie or Wyatt. The woods rang with the bellowed calls of searchers until late afternoon, when most of them straggled back to the main house to renew themselves with food and dry clothing before setting out once again.

No one suspected that Cassie would have been so close to the main house, least of all Wyatt, and for that reason, she went totally undetected. A small, ragged strip of white cloth had been found snagged on a thorn at that point where Cassie had finally turned back from her headlong plunge into the forest, and the pattern of the search ranged outward from that focal point. It was there that the searchers began calling her name, never imagining that she was nearly a mile behind them, and well out of earshot of their first calls.

Cassie didn't recall falling asleep, and she couldn't pinpoint what sense had alerted her, but she came awake with a start, and with the absolute certainty that night was falling, and she was not alone.

'Hello?' she called out timidly, amazed to hear the faint squeak that came from her raw throat. 'Is anyone there?' she forced out more loudly.

She sat perfectly still, her head cocked and her ears straining to catch any sound. She heard the muted chirps and flutters of birds settling for the night, the steady drips of water falling from leaves to splash on the soggy carpet around her, and something else. A sound so restrained and controlled it was barely audible—the sound of human breathing.

'Here!' she cried out weakly with relief. 'I'm here!' But there was no answering call, no footsteps rushing towards her, and now even the breathing seemed to have stopped.

Cassie frowned anxiously, listening to the silence that followed her cry, doubting her senses. There *was* someone there. There had to be. She couldn't have been so wrong. Unless—unless she had been dreaming; groggy from sleep, and had only imagined something she wanted so desperately to hear.

She fingered the face of her watch and read 8:15. Surely they would be looking for her? She'd been gone since morning, in one of the worst storms she'd ever experienced. They must be looking.

'Wyatt!' she called as loudly as she could, but the cry was only a croak from her overused throat. It served only to remind her of his indifferent rejection that morning, and the memory washed over her in a wave of anguish. He had only been part of her life for a matter of days, yet now she could not imagine a life without him. It stretched endlessly, emptily before her, and she felt a sharp, physical pain where she imagined her heart to be.

And then she heard it. The crack of a twig snapping under a weight just a few yards in front of her and, simultaneously, a current of air that carried a faint fragrance to her nostrils. She broke into a smile and extended one hand, all thoughts of Wyatt shelved temporarily in the gush of relief at being rescued. 'Helen,' she whispered weakly. 'Thank God.'

But Helen didn't answer. Nor did she accept the outstretched hand, yet Cassie knew she was there. The perfume, faint though it was, was unmistakably hers, as were the footsteps that were now treading stealthily away, deeper into the forest.

Away? The realisation slapped Cassie from weak

relief to a state of astonishment, and her eyes widened in disbelief. She was walking away!

'Helen!' she tried to scream, but the cry was an agonised whisper.

Why? she thought. Why would she leave her?

She had no way of knowing that Helen had never had any intention of helping in the search; that she had only skirted the edge of the woods in a sullen attempt to give the pretence of searching, while hoping fervently that Cassie had been crushed by one of the hundreds of trees that had fallen victim to the storm. It would serve her right.

She had come to Windrow and within a day's time had captured the attention of a man Helen had longed for secretly for years. His polite indifference to her had been an ongoing disappointment, but Helen had been able to accept that, as long as no one else achieved what she had not. But then Cassie Winters appeared, and Helen had recognised the emotion in Wyatt's eyes, long before he had acknowledged it himself, and her resentment of Cassie was born.

Spoiled, weak, helpless rich girl! Pampered for years, her life filled with the material comforts Helen would never know, now threatening to remove the one solace she clung to in her drab, empty existence.

Day after day she had watched the rigid distance of a man who shared her own cool reserve melt into an insipid longing for this colourless creature, and there was nothing she could do to prevent it. Her rage was boundless.

She had been as startled to come upon Cassie huddled in sleep behind the tree as Cassie had been to sense her presence, and the disappointment to find her unharmed had been bitter. And though the conscious thought of doing serious physical harm never occured to her, she refused to play heroine and lead the despicable blind girl back to safety. That would have been too much to ask. And so she simply walked away, lost in her own morose depression, oblivious to the pathetic cries that followed her. Let her find her own way out. Or let someone else find her, and it was inevitable that they find her soon. But it didn't have to be her.

Cassie scrambled after the faint sounds of Helen's retreat desperately, afraid to call out again for fear of masking the noise of Helen's passage through the heavy underbrush. If Helen would not help her, as incredible as that might be, at least she could follow her back to Windrow and safety.

But her legs had fallen asleep in their tucked position; grown stiff with hours of immobility and cold; and Helen was far ahead by the time Cassie's sluggish circulation had brought life back to the rigid limbs. Her attempts to hurry were thwarted by the obstacles that tripped her again and again, and she was soon ragged and filthy from her many falls on to the soggy ground.

She paused briefly at the top of an incline to listen. Her face and hands were covered with dozens of angry scratches from her battles with thorns and branches. Bright drops of red seeped from some of the wounds, but all were superficial, and she was numbed to the tiny pains as she strained to hear the sound of human footsteps. Her eyes were directed straight ahead, her concentration fiercely intense, when between her shaky gasps for breath she finally heard what she had been waiting for: the crack of a dead twig as it was snapped from a bush.

'Helen!' she cried hoarsely, and her right foot took a step forward and came down on nothing but air.

She was not to know that the twig she had heard snap had buckled under the weight of a surprised sparrow; that the bird had attempted to perch for the night on the uppermost growth of an ancient tree that stretched for light from its berth in a ravine fifty feet deep; that Helen was nearly half a mile behind her, crossing the back lawn towards Windrow's main house.

She knew only that she was tumbling head over heels down a steep slope, smashing young bushes with the force of her sliding weight, grasping at grasses, or rocky soil, or whatever would give her hands purchase to slow the bruising rush of the fall. She slid, rolled, and bounced downward until her body came to an abrupt stop against the petrified corpse of an elm long-since ravaged by disease. The back of her head struck the rock-hard trunk with a dull thud, and she marvelled at the pinpoints of light that appeared before her eyes just before she slipped into unconsciousness. The lights wavered and danced and merged into a single, bright circle, then faded away.

Over a mile away, deeper into the woods than even hunters ever bothered to venture, Wyatt plodded steadily forward, following the broken trail of a storm-crazed deer, thinking it might be Cassie's. He was nearing the twelfth hour of a fruitless, desperate search, broken twice by hopeful returns to the house, only to be discouraged by the solemn head-shaking of Maggie, or Katy, or Matt. The Franklins had rushed to Windrow as soon as they had heard the news, and it was Katy who had bundled Wyatt in Matt's cotton-lined raincoat, stuffing the pockets with candy bars, and who had forced him to swallow every drop of a tall glass of orange juice before allowing him to leave again. She had blanched at his sallow complexion, at the scratches on his face and hands, and most of all, at the hollow emptiness of his gaze, but she said nothing. She knew his body was well past exhaustion, but understood that it was in far better condition than the mind behind those eyes, and that the only remedy for that anguish was continuing the search.

The destruction in the forest had terrified him. Even though he had lumbered blindly through the worst of the storm, hearing the trees crack and fall around him, the driving rain had hidden the worst of the damage. It was later, in the dripping calm afterward, that he saw how many trees had crashed to the ground; how many jagged trunks still smoked from the electric kiss of lightning; and realised how improbable it would be to find Cassie unscathed by the storm's fury.

He searched doggedly, his eyes sharp with dread, his face tight with the ache of worrying that at any moment, he might find her broken body pinned under one of the hundreds of fallen trees.

CHAPTER FOURTEEN

IN the black hours that followed her plummeting fall into the ravine, Cassie slipped in and out of consciousness, dimly aware of the passage of time and of the night sounds of the forest. She jerked to full, painful wakefulness at one point, and the realisation that Helen had left her to die hit her with stunning, merciless clarity. Her mind recoiled against the frightening admission that anyone would leave a helpless human being to die, refusing to believe it possible, and she whimpered in the night, startling a family of racoons into a hasty, scurrying retreat from the ravine floor.

Weak from hunger and thirst and cold, dizzy still from the blow to her head, her thoughts clouded with fever and she slipped mercifully into a semi-conscious state.

Her mother called to her sharply, and she frowned in her delirium. Her mother never raised her voice, certainly never shouted, but there it was, all the same. That harsh, strident scream, still plainly her mother's voice, shrieking, 'Get down, Cassie! Get down!' And then it was hard to breathe, and she knew somehow it was because her face was pressed into her mother's lap while her mother hovered over her, shielding her, and there was a grinding screech and a terrible impact and the long scream of metal tearing against metal that finally died in a puff of black smoke. She seemed to wake in her dream, struggling through a fog, pushing frantically at a weight pressing down on her, and then she sat erect and looked at her mother slumped against her. That lovely, beloved face was serene as always, though marred by a tiny trickle of blood that seeped from between her lips, spoiling the perfection of the fair skin. There was a large discoloration on the smooth forehead, and even though she was only a child in her dream, she knew her mother was gone. She shook her head wildly in the throes of a nightmare she could not escape, and then she grew still, numbed by shock, and only the bright flames of yellow and orange penetrated her stupor.

Still dreaming, she saw tiny hands struggle to lift the old-fashioned handle of a jammed car door, saw tiny fists pounding against an expanse of smoky glass, and in her dream, and in reality, she began to scream for her father.

Wyatt was stumbling back through the woods towards the main house when he heard the first scream. He jerked rigidly erect and caught his breath, his eyes snapping shut immediately to focus all attention to his ears.

Again, he prayed fervently, his lips forming the silent words. Again, again, scream again.

And she did. It was the high, piercing wail of a child, splitting the night air with a terror so sharp that a chill ran down his spine in that instant before he spun around and began to run.

'Daddy!' The voice that was Cassie's and yet not Cassie's cried frantically, pathetically, over and over again, growing weaker with each effort. 'Daddy! Daddy. Daddy ... Dad ...'

Wyatt plunged through underbrush, pushing aside the brambles that left unfelt scratches on his arms; running, running, faster and faster, heedless of the roots that grasped at his ankles, of the dangers of dashing headlong through a maze of bent and twisted trees, intent on only one thing: reaching the fading voice before he lost it, before he lost *her*; and then he was at the lip of the ravine, staring down at the huddled, writhing form, calling her name once before plunging down the slope in a sliding rush of flying stones and dirt.

He knelt next to her silently, warily; his heart constricted with the fear that he may be too late. For she was suddenly quiet, and still.

'Cassie,' he whispered desperately as he gazed at her inert form, his heart thudding with first hope, and then dread. Then he reached out tentatively to touch a large bruise on her cheek. She moved slightly and whimpered, and the sagging relief that swept through his body, pulling him down, down with its weight, was shattered by her final scream.

'DADDY!'

He jerked upright in terror, shouting, 'Cassie! Wake up!' forgetting in the panic of the moment everything he had ever learned about psychiatry, forgetting that she was where he had wanted her to be from the beginning; back there—back in the past, seeing the horror that had kept her blind; knowing only that he loved her, and that all that mattered was sparing her the fear and the terror and the sudden, dreadful knowledge that sat like an ugly demon upon her face.

'Wake up, wake up; God, please, wake up,' he whispered urgently, but Cassie shook her head strongly and he watched her slipping away, back there, back where he couldn't help her.

Cassie was still in the car; still trapped by the jammed door and the acrid smoke; still enclosed in the suffocating tomb of a nightmare that would not stop. And the worst was yet to come. She could feel it coming, bearing down; feel the desperate flutter of a seven-year-old heart panicking in a tiny, helpless seven-year-old body, and the body was hers.

She didn't want to lift her eyes and squint against the smoke to look out the car window. She knew she was supposed to do that, that she *would* do that, but she fought against it, jerking her head from side to side in delirious denial, moaning, squeezing her eyes shut tight. But it didn't help. Her mind looked out of the car window, just as she had looked years before, and she saw the horror she had locked away long ago, and it was her father. He stood rigidly away from the car, watching his only child pound impotent little fists against the walls of her fiery prison, his eyes wide with shock and fear, and he made no move to help her.

Cassie's fists pounded on Wyatt's chest as he held her, and when she began to whimper, he strained to hear her words, powerless to do anything else.

'It's hot, Daddy! It's hot! Let me out! Hurry, Daddy! Let me out! Why don't you move, Daddy? Why don't you let me out? Why are you just standing there?'

Wyatt's eyes widened as the realisation of what the words meant struck him, his face drawn with the horror of what he heard, knowing at last the awful secret a child's mind had locked away. 'Dear God,' he breathed, letting the horror give way to anger; a twisted, blistering anger against a dead man he wanted to kill.

Suddenly Cassie quieted in his arms, and Wyatt watched as her face stilled with the final acceptance of a bewildered five-year-old child, watching her father as he watched her die.

In her dream, as she had been in life on that fateful night, Cassie was numbed by shock and smoke inhalation by the time the uniformed man rushed to the car, tore the door nearly off its hinges, swept her into his arms and ran. But she could still hear the ragged, frantic gasps of his breathing, still feel the urgent pounding of his heart as he clutched her close and ran past the immobile, staring form of her father. And then there was the deafening roar of an explosion behind them, and the force broke in a wave of hot air that flung the officer to the ground on top of her, and everything went black.

She cried in her dream through tightly closed eyes, feeling the comfort and the safety of the policeman's arms around her; hearing him murmur her name over and over again as he stroked her hair. It was a dream, and it was the truth, and her weeping built to racking sobs that shook her shoulders with their force, for the truth of her father's failure had been terrible.

And then she came up from the hideous fog of her nightmare, and realised that the policeman didn't know her name; that he couldn't, and that it was Wyatt's voice, and Wyatt's arms, and at last, she was safe.

'Wyatt?' she murmured incredulously into his chest.

'Yes, Cassie,' he whispered, wrapping her more tightly in his embrace.

'Oh, Wyatt!' she sobbed, trying to lift limp arms to wrap around his neck.

'It's all right, Cassie. I'm here. I'll always be here.'

She shuddered once, then pressed her face against him. 'I saw it,' she trembled. 'I saw it all. It was my father . . . all the time, it was my father . . .'

His touch was incredibly gentle as he caressed the back of her head, and he steeled himself for what he had to do. He knew that the dream had not been enough; that she would have to say it aloud to banish the nightmare forever. And that was his job, after all; to bring old ghosts out into the open and heal the wounds, so he made himself ask the questions, though he already knew the answers.

'What did you see, Cassie?' he asked gently. 'What did your father do?'

The tears ran unchecked between her closed lids, and her body jerked spasmodically as she gasped for air between the sobs. When there were no more tears left, she spoke against the soggy fabric of his shirt, moving only her lips, and her voice was dull and lifeless.

'He just stood there,' she whispered. 'He just stood there, watching me die. My God! How could he do that?' She shook her head against the memory, and when she spoke again, her voice was faint, almost musing. 'He looked so . . . strange . . . just standing there . . . watching, staring . . . as if he didn't see me at all . . .'

And then suddenly Wyatt could see the man behind his closed eyelids, standing there rigid with shock.

watching his life go up in flames before his eyes, but not seeing it at all; and though there would never be forgiveness for what the man had done, he began to understand.

'He *didn't* see you, Cassie. You have to believe that!' he hissed into her hair. 'Fear, Cassie; adult fear. It's the strongest emotion there is. It blocks out everything else. Your father was in shock. *He wasn't seeing anything.*'

Cassie lay still, listening to the words, wanting to believe, knowing that for her own sake, she had to learn to pity the man who was her father, and not hate him.

'It was only afterwards, Cassie,' the gentle voice went on, 'that he realised what he had done. And the guilt must have been terrible. I don't know how he lived with it. I suppose he thought he had to—for your sake—as little as he may have been, he was all you had left.'

'And that's why he liked me blind,' she said bitterly. 'As long as I stayed blind, it meant I didn't remember.'

'Because he couldn't have lived with that, Cassie; don't you see? He could never have faced you again, if you remembered how he failed you.'

She took a deep, shuddering breath, and tried to stop the tears, but they came again anyway, washing away the pain and the hurt, mourning the man she thought was her father; accepting at last the man he really was.

Wyatt buried his face in her neck, sharing her pain, lessening it somehow, pulling her back from the past. She felt the warmth of his arms, and his breath on her neck, and let everything else slip away, feeling at last the deep, secure knowledge that she was loved.

Then her eyes fluttered open and she froze instantly, looking at a world she could see for the first time in eighteen years.

'What is it?' he asked, feeling her body stiffen, lifting his head to look down at her face. 'Where does it hurt?' Then his eyes narrowed in puzzlement at the rapt, wide-eyed countenance that looked up at him, lips parted in a wondering smile.

She looked directly into the clear, blue eyes she had

imagined a thousand times, beyond them to the tousled, rain-soaked black curls, the wonderfully strong lines of his face, now softened with concern, marred with dozens of angry scratches and the haunted expression of a man who had nearly lost everything. A face she had never seen; yet achingly, dearly familiar.

'You need a shave,' she whispered, and his face cleared as she watched, stiffening into a rigid mask of amazed disbelief.

'You can see . . .' he said tonelessly, and it was a statement of fact, not a question. 'You can see.'

She smiled up at him, drinking in the sight of his face, reaching out to brush her fingers across the black stubble that shadowed his cheek, saying nothing.

He released her abruptly then, stood, and turned away. Cassie pushed herself weakly to a sitting position, and stared with wonder at the back of the man she loved and had never seen.

His voice was stern, covering, she knew, the depths of his emotion. 'Well,' he said harshly, still turned away from her, 'you managed to create quite an uproar. The entire staff and every deputy in the county has been looking for you since yesterday.'

He paused and she watched him lift a hand forward and lean heavily against a tree. Her eyes lingered on the black, tousled curls as he bent his head, then dropped to the shoulders that hunched strangely for a moment before he spoke again. 'Where have you been, anyway?' he demanded, and she almost laughed at the foolishness of the question. What did it matter now, and how would a blind woman know where she had been?

He leaned against the tree for a long time, neither moving nor speaking. Cassie saw his arm quiver with the pressure of his hand pressed against the trunk; watched his fingers tighten around the raised bark until his knuckles were white.

'It was a stupid thing to do!' he spat out finally. 'A childish thing to do! Running off with a storm coming, worrying everybody . . .'

'Everybody?' she asked softly.

Then he turned back to look down at her, and she could see everything there on his face, and wondered if it had always been there. He bent quickly and crouched over her, and she reached out to touch his lips with one finger.

'I think this is the part when you look deep into my eyes, and then kiss me,' she said quietly.

The corner of his mouth twitched. 'Is it now?' he asked, and his voice trembled.

'Yes it is. And then you'll admit that you've loved me all along, and we'll get right down to the subject at hand, which is when we're going to get married.'

'Really.' The twitch had grown to a half-smile.

'Yes, really. Can you support me, Wyatt, while I learn to do something? Unless you're very rich, of course. That's all I know how to be, you know, is a very rich lady.'

'Lucky for you Ms Winters,' he smiled, 'that I'm a very rich man.'

She cocked her head slightly and frowned. 'Are you really? I didn't know that . . .' Then she yawned and smiled all at the same time.

He touched her brow tenderly with one hand, then slid his arms beneath her and rose effortlessly to his feet. She snuggled against his chest as he began the slow climb out of the ravine, listening to the strong beat of his heart under her ear.

'Wyatt?' she mumbled softly, her voice strained and tired.

'Hmmm?'

'Is your house big enough for a housekeeper?'

'Yes,' he smiled. 'Easily.'

'Good. Then Mrs Carmody can come to live with us. That's all right with you, isn't it?' She yawned again and nestled deeper into his arms.

'Yes, Cassie,' he whispered, bending his head and pressing his lips to her hair. 'That's all right with me.' He chuckled softly then, and tightened his arms around her. 'But you're taking a lot for granted, aren't you? I haven't even told you how much I love you yet.'

'You don't have to,' she smiled, opening her eyes one more time to make sure the world was still there. 'I'd have to be blind not to see that.'

Coming Next Month in Harlequin Presents!

855 A FOREVER AFFAIR Rosemary Carter
Despite its savage beauty, her husband's African game reserve is no longer home. Was it carved in stone that she could never love another man? Surely a divorce would change that!

856 PROMISE OF THE UNICORN Sara Craven
To collect on a promise, a young woman returns her talisman—the protector of virgins—to its original owner. The power of the little glass unicorn was now with him!

857 AN IRRESISTIBLE FORCE Ann Charlton
A young woman is in danger of being taken over by a subtle irresistible force rather than by open aggression when she takes on an Australian construction king who's trying to buy out her grandmother.

858 INNOCENT PAWN Catherine George
Instead of looking past the money to the man behind it, a mother is prompted to panic to blame her husband when their five-year-old daughter is kidnapped.

859 MALIBU MUSIC Rosemary Hammond
California sunshine and her sister's beach house provide the atmosphere a young woman needs to focus on her future—until her neighbor tries to seduce her.

860 LADY SURRENDER Carole Mortimer
The man who bursts into her apartment can't see why his best friend would throw away his marriage for a woman like her. But soon he can't imagine any man—married or otherwise—*not* falling for her.

861 A MODEL OF DECEPTION Margaret Pargeter
A model takes on an assignment she can't handle when she tries to entice a man into selling his island in the Caribbean. She was supposed to deceive the man, not fall in love.

862 THE HAWK OF VENICE Sally Wentworth
Most people travel to Venice to fall in love. Instead, an au pair girl makes the journey to accuse a respected Venetian count of kidnapping—or of seduction, at least.

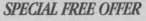

Here's how to get this special offer from Harlequin!

SEPTEMBER
TREASURY EDITION
COUPON

As simple as 1…2…3!

1. Each month, save one Treasury Edition coupon from your favorite Romance or Presents novel.
2. In four months you'll have saved four Treasury Edition coupons (<u>only one coupon per month allowed</u>).
3. Then all you have to do is fill out and return the order form provided, along with the four Treasury Edition coupons required and $1.00 for postage and handling.

Mail to: Harlequin Reader Service

In the U.S.A.
2504 West Southern Ave.
Tempe, AZ 85282

In Canada
P.O. Box 2800, Postal Station A
5170 Yonge Street
Willowdale, Ont. M2N 6J3

RT1-B-2

Please send me my FREE copy of the Janet Dailey Treasury Edition. I have enclosed the four Treasury Edition coupons required and $1.00 for postage and handling along with this order form.

(Please Print)

NAME_____

ADDRESS_____

CITY_____

STATE/PROV._____ ZIP/POSTAL CODE_____

SIGNATURE_____

This offer is limited to one order per household.

This special Janet Dailey offer expires January 1986.

SUPPLIES LIMITED

EYE OF THE STORM

MAURA SEGER

A powerful portrayal of the events of World War II in the Pacific, *Eye of the Storm* is a riveting story of how love triumphs over hatred. In this, the first of a three-book chronicle, Army nurse Maggie Lawrence meets Marine Sgt. Anthony Gargano. Despite military regulations against fraternization, they resolve to face together whatever lies ahead.... Author Maura Seger, also known to her fans as Laurel Winslow, Sara Jennings, Anne MacNeil and Jenny Bates, was named 1984's Most Versatile Romance Author by *The Romantic Times*.

EYE-E-1R

Take 4 novels and a surprise gift FREE

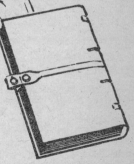